Praise for the first book in
Dixie Browning's
THE LAWLESS HEIRS miniseries,
The Passionate G-Man…

"Dixie Browning wonderfully deepens an attraction of opposites into a strong and beautiful love in this freshly appealing romance."

—*Romantic Times Magazine*

And praise for Dixie Browning…

"There is no one writing romance today who touches the heart and tickles the ribs like Dixie Browning. The people in her books are as warm and real as a sunbeam and just as lovely."

—*New York Times* bestselling author Nora Roberts

* * *

"Dixie Browning has given the romance industry years of love and laughter in her wonderful books."

—*New York Times* bestselling author Linda Howard

* * *

"Each of Dixie's books is a keeper guaranteed to warm the heart and delight the senses."

—*New York Times* bestselling author Jayne Ann Krentz

* * *

"A true pioneer in romantic fiction, the delightful Dixie Browning is a reader's most precious treasure, a constant source of outstanding entertainment."

—*Romantic Times Magazine*

* * *

"Dixie's books never disappoint—they always lift your spirit!"

—*USA Today* bestselling author Mary Lynn Baxter

Dear Reader,

Happy Valentine's Day! And what better way to celebrate Cupid's reign than by reading six brand-new Desire novels...?

Putting us in the mood for sensuous love is this February's MAN OF THE MONTH, with wonderful Dixie Browning offering us the final title in her THE LAWLESS HEIRS miniseries in *A Knight in Rusty Armor.* This alpha-male hero knows just what to do when faced with a sultry damsel in distress!

Continue to follow the popular Fortune family's romances in the Desire series FORTUNE'S CHILDREN: THE BRIDES. The newest installment, *Society Bride* by Elizabeth Bevarly, features a spirited debutante who runs away from a business-deal marriage…into the arms of the rugged rancher of her dreams.

Ever-talented Anne Marie Winston delivers the second story in her BUTLER COUNTY BRIDES, with a single mom opening her home and heart to a seductive acquaintance, in *Dedicated to Deirdre.* Then a modern-day cowboy renounces his footloose ways for love in *The Outlaw Jesse James,* the final title in Cindy Gerard's OUTLAW HEARTS miniseries; while a child's heartwarming wish for a father is granted in Raye Morgan's *Secret Dad.* And with *Little Miss Innocent?* Lori Foster proves that opposites *do* attract.

This Valentine's Day, Silhouette Desire's little red books sizzle with compelling romance and make the perfect gift for the contemporary woman—you! So treat yourself to all six!

Enjoy!

Joan Marlow Golan
Senior Editor, Silhouette Desire

DIXIE BROWNING

A KNIGHT IN RUSTY ARMOR

SILHOUETTE BOOKS

ISBN 0-373-76195-3

A KNIGHT IN RUSTY ARMOR

This edition published by arrangement with Harlequin Books S.A.

Printed in U.S.A.

Books by Dixie Browning

Silhouette Desire

Shadow of Yesterday #68
Image of Love #91
The Hawk and the Honey #111
Late Rising Moon #121
Stormwatch #169
The Tender Barbarian #188
Matchmaker's Moon #212
A Bird in the Hand #234
In the Palm of Her Hand #264
A Winter Woman #324
There Once Was a Lover #337
Fate Takes a Holiday #403
Along Came Jones #427
Thin Ice #474
Beginner's Luck #517
Ships in the Night #541
Twice in a Blue Moon #588
Just Say Yes #637
Not a Marrying Man #678
Gus and the Nice Lady #691
Best Man for the Job #720
Hazards of the Heart #780
Kane's Way #801
Keegan's Hunt #820
Lucy and the Stone #853
Two Hearts, Slightly Used #890
†*Alex and the Angel* #949
†*The Beauty, the Beast and the Baby* #985
The Baby Notion #1011
†*Stryker's Wife* #1033
Look What the Stork Brought #1111
‡*The Passionate G-Man* #1141
‡*A Knight in Rusty Armor* #1195

Silhouette Yours Truly

Single Female (Reluctantly) Seeks...

*Outer Banks
†Tall, Dark and Handsome
‡The Lawless Heirs

Silhouette Special Edition

Finders Keepers #50
Reach Out To Cherish #110
Just Deserts #181
Time and Tide #205
By Any Other Name #228
The Security Man #314
Belonging #414

Silhouette Romance

Unreasonable Summer #12
Tumbled Wall #38
Chance Tomorrow #53
Wren of Paradise #73
East of Today #93
Winter Blossom #113
Renegade Player #142
Island on the Hill #164
Logic of the Heart #172
Loving Rescue #191
A Secret Valentine #203
Practical Dreamer #221
Visible Heart #275
Journey to Quiet Waters #292
The Love Thing #305
First Things Last #323
Something for Herself #381
Reluctant Dreamer #460
A Matter of Timing #527
The Homing Instinct #747

Silhouette Books

Silhouette Christmas Stories 1987
"Henry the Ninth"

Spring Fancy 1994
"Grace and the Law"

World's Most Eligible Bachelors
His Business, Her Baby

DIXIE BROWNING

celebrated her sixtieth book for Silhouette with the publication of *Stryker's Wife* in 1996. She has also written a number of historical romances with her sister under the name Bronwyn Williams. A charter member of Romance Writers of America, and a member of Novelists, Inc., Browning has won numerous awards for her work. She divides her time between Winston-Salem and the Outer Banks of North Carolina.

One

Travis Holiday eased off the accelerator as he hit another patch of sand, this one even deeper than the last. He'd hoped to get home before dark. Not that it mattered. He could have stayed away a year and it wouldn't have mattered. There was a lot to be said for living alone, where a man could go and come with a minimum of hassle.

Waylon and Willie launched into the one about being on the road again, and Trav hummed along, his pleasant baritone only slightly off-key. With his fist, he cleared a circle on the steamy inside of his windshield. It didn't help much. The outside was clouded with salt and pitted from years of beach driving.

"On the ro-oad again..." Off-key or not, he kept perfect time with the wipers. Waylon and Willie lagged about half a beat behind.

In spite of the worsening weather, the day had gone

a lot better than he'd expected. Not that he'd been expecting much, but the cousin he'd never even heard of until a few months ago had turned out to be a pretty decent guy.

Considering the difference in their backgrounds, they'd hit it off surprisingly well. Hell, they even looked alike. Same build. Same general coloring. Same plain, angular features.

Lately, he'd thought a lot about family. About roots. He'd never wasted much time thinking about that sort of thing before. The little he knew about his parents had been more than enough.

But things were different now that he had a son. Once he'd gotten past the shock, he'd started thinking in terms of a heritage. Of what it meant to be a living link between past and future. If his son had children, and those children had children—

"What the bloody—!" He slammed on the brakes, swearing as the pickup slid dangerously close to the edge of the narrow highway and came to a stop. Rolling down the window, he leaned his head out to peer through the mixture of rain, blowing sand and salt spray. Didn't that damned fool know better than to park in the middle of the road?

But he didn't yell. Didn't even hit the horn. If there was one thing twenty years in the Coast Guard taught a man, it was the importance of discipline. Even when some cheese-for-brains idiot parked on the centerline, completely blocking the narrow highway.

He watched for a full minute while a crazy woman launched an all-out attack on the car, a yellow, vinyl-topped clunker. It wasn't the first time Travis Holiday had seen a tire being kicked. It was, however, the first time he'd seen a car being flogged to death with a ladies' shoulder bag.

Not that he could blame her, if the thing had conked out on her with no warning in the middle of a storm with night coming on fast.

Pulling his own vehicle as far off the highway as possible, Trav switched off the engine, zipped up his sheepskin-lined leather jacket, battled the wind for possession of the door and climbed out of the high cab. Crazy or not, this was no place for a woman alone. Hatteras Island was safer than most places, especially this time of year when there were few strangers around, but even so…

''Ma'am?'' Either she didn't hear him or she chose to ignore him. Squinting against the wet, gale-force winds that screamed in off the Atlantic, he gave it another try.

He was no more than a few yards away when she turned to confront him. He'd seen the look before, having done his share of search-and-rescue missions. Shock, stress, stark terror—he'd seen it all.

What he saw this time was wild, wet hair blowing in the wind, a thin face that was ghost pale except for a pair of big, red-rimmed eyes and a red-tipped nose. She didn't look too thrilled at being rescued.

''Listen, lady, you can't—'' She took a tighter grip on her purse. Good God, did she think he was after her money? ''Ma'am, nobody's going to hurt you.'' He held up his hands, palms out, to let her knew he wasn't armed. Hell, she was more dangerous than he was, the way she was swinging that leather sack of hers. ''Ma'am, you don't need to be out here in this mess. You're getting soaked.''

She was not only soaking wet, she was crying. Either

that or she'd got sand in her eyes. She sucked in air and swallowed hard. Trav could actually see her throat working. There was an emergency blanket under the seat of his truck, but he wasn't too eager to turn his back on her. She might even take a notion to walk off into the ocean. He'd seen crazier reactions from people in a severe state of shock.

She continued to stare at him. He stared right back, trying to infuse the look with reassurance. Trying to look benign, harmless, helpful.

It obviously wasn't working. "Ma'am? Are you okay?"

Stupid question. Her bottom lip trembled, and he swore under his breath. *Lady, don't do this to me.* He retreated a step, then stood his ground, braced in case she hurled herself into his arms. It was a dumb idea, one that came and went in a split second—something about the way she was looking at him.

But she didn't budge, and neither did he. What with all the crap blowing in the air, he told himself he must have misinterpreted the fleeting look on her face. It wouldn't be the first time he'd misread a woman's intentions.

"Ma'am, you shouldn't stop in the middle of the highway. With dark coming on, you could get rammed."

She went right on staring at him. Didn't say a word, didn't even blink.

"One way or another," he said, feigning patience, "we're going to have to get your car off the road. Do you think you can steer if I push?"

Finally, something got through. He let out a gust of relief as she cautiously lowered the purse she'd been holding as if it were part shield, part weapon. "Of course I can steer. Will you use your truck?"

"Probably be the best way," he said, careful not to sound sarcastic. What did she think he was going to do, break his back trying to shove a ton and a half of junk metal off the road manually? "We're going to have a problem with the bumpers. I'll try to go easy, but you might end up with a dent on your rear end."

As if one more scar on that battered old carcass would make any difference in her blue-book value, which would be about a buck ninety-nine, tops.

"What do you want me to do?"

"Get in, take her out of gear, and once you feel me engage your backside, steer as far over to the right as you can without going off onto the shoulder. You can't see it now, but there's about three feet of paved bicycle path underneath the sand. Try your best to stay on it, okay?"

She nodded, but didn't make a move. Trav shrugged, stepped past her to open the door. Once she got in, he scooped the long, flapping tail of her wet coat out of the way and slammed the door shut.

Cashmere, he thought. He was no expert, but he'd lay odds the coat she was wearing was cashmere. He hoped to hell it was warmer than it looked. The temperature was in the high thirties, but with the rain and the wind-chill factor, it must be somewhere near zilch.

His bumper made contact about halfway up her trunk. It was going to do some damage, but a car coming over the dune at high speed would do considerably more. Even if he got her off the road, there was no guarantee her car would be here by the time a tow truck could get up the beach, what with the wind, the tide and the drifting sand.

Gently he pushed the elderly, banana-colored four-door far enough over to the edge that another vehicle could pass. He waited, and when the woman didn't climb out again he went and opened her door. "Ma'am, you can't stay here. Tide's on the way in. With the wind out of the northeast, I can't let you risk it. I'll drive you wherever you're headed and call the garage for your car."

Not that he held out much hope of getting a tow truck out before morning, but if he was any judge, the sooner she reached her destination, got out of those wet clothes and into something warm and dry, the better off she'd be, he thought as he helped her into his passenger seat.

Unless he was very much mistaken, she was one sick puppy. She kept swallowing. From the way she winced, Trav figured it was a pretty painful process.

Tooling south along the narrow stretch of beach, he shot her a worried glance from time to time. There wasn't enough light to take in many details, but he didn't need to. Having recently retired after a twenty-year career, he had filed his last report. Still, some habits were hard to break, so he mentally filed away a few particulars.

Age? Probably somewhere between thirty-five and forty-five. Eyes, gray. Or possibly a dull shade of blue or green—it was hard to tell in this light. Definitely red-rimmed, though. As for her nose, it was short, straight, narrow, red and shiny. Prominent cheekbones, but that might be just the shadowy hollows underneath.

She was thin. Skinny, in fact. He was no expert on the female form, but she reminded him of the way a high-fashion model might look after a weeklong binge of dieting.

He had a feeling there was more to her story than that.

He also had a feeling he didn't want to hear it.

Trav was Coast Guard. Retirement couldn't change a lifetime of tradition, not to mention conditioning. If he came across someone who needed rescuing, he did the job. But that didn't mean he had to take on their personal problems. He had enough of those himself.

''Where're you headed?'' She must be a local. This time of year, tourists were a rare species. Or in this case, an endangered species.

She named a restaurant in Hatteras village on the far end of the island. He'd never eaten there, but he'd heard it was pretty good.

''I'm not sure,'' he said cautiously, ''but I think it might be shut down for the winter.''

''I've been offered a job there.''

A job. Right. He didn't know who she was, much less what she was doing here, but he did know that waitresses didn't usually turn up out of season wearing cashmere coats, looking feverish and hungry and lost. ''You're sure about that? Not much business down here this time of year.''

''Just take me there. If it's not out of the way. Please.''

Oh, hell. If he had good sense he'd drop her off at the doctor's office— only the island's doctor was down with the flu, as he'd found out yesterday when he'd driven an elderly neighbor to his office for a routine checkup.

''Who's your contact at the restaurant?'' From the look she gave him, he might as well have been speaking Mandarin. ''I mean, who hired you? Are they expecting you? I can give 'em a call.''

She was hoarse. What he'd taken as a soft, sexy drawl sounded painful to him now that he'd had time to size her up better. She had one hell of a cold, if that's all it was.

He'd better hope that's all it was. He'd put off having a flu shot this year until he figured it was too late to do any good. The last thing he needed now was one more hitch in his plans.

She pulled an address book from her purse and read off a number. He punched it in his cell phone, and they both heard the message on the other end. "Sorry, we're closed for the season. See you in April."

"Oh," she said plaintively, and he resisted the urge to lay a comforting hand on her shoulder. These days, a man couldn't be too careful. She thumbed through her book. "Could you try this number?"

He tried it, only to be rewarded with another recording. An irritatingly cheerful woman's voice came on with, "Leave a message, hon—I'll get back to you sooner or later. Surf's up."

Yeah, sure it was. God, he hated flippant messages.

By then they'd entered Buxton village and were within a quarter of a mile of his house. The last thing he wanted was to take her home with him. His house wasn't even finished, much less furnished. He'd been more or less camping out there while he put up paneling in what would be Matthew's room once he could get his ex-wife to let the boy come east.

The lady was shivering again. He had his heater cranked up to the max. He'd already shed his coat, and sweat was trickling down his throat, but he'd figured she'd be chilled—what with the wet clothes and all. No telling how long she'd been standing out in the rain, beating a dead horse.

Or in this case, a dead sedan.

''Look, I'm going to take you to my house until we can track down your friend, okay? By the way, my name's Travis Holiday.'' She looked at him dully, so he tacked on a few credentials, figuring it might reassure her. ''Lieutenant Commander, retired, U.S. Coast Guard. Uh…I could call somebody to stay with you if it would make you feel more comfortable.''

Right. His nearest neighbor was Miss Cal, who was arthritic, pushing ninety and had a tongue like a whipsaw. Except for a stone-deaf sheepdog named Skye and a few yard chickens, she lived alone.

He didn't think either Skye or his mistress were going to be much help in this situation.

''Do you have any aspirin?'' the woman croaked.

Aspirin. He had a feeling she needed more than that. Like maybe a full brain transplant. ''Yeah, sure—at home. I'll make you something hot to drink when we get there, and then we'll try again to contact your friend.''

Ruanna had probably felt worse, but at the moment she couldn't remember when. She'd been driving since yesterday, feeling sicker with every mile. If she could have afforded a longer stay in the cheap motel where she'd spent last night, she'd have slept until she either recovered—or didn't. The alternative had been to get to Moselle's place before she collapsed, only her car had collapsed first.

Once she'd crossed Oregon Inlet, traffic had all but disappeared. Even before that she'd begun to suspect that whatever bug she'd picked up, her car had caught it, too, but by then there was nothing to do but keep going, hoping they'd both last a few more miles.

She'd filled up the tank in Manteo. Not even her old guzzler could guzzle that fast, but when it had started to cough in a way that suggested it wasn't getting enough fuel, she'd slowed down and watched for a service station. The first two stations she'd passed had been closed, and she'd foolishly gambled on making it to the next village.

And then her car had coughed twice and died, right there in the middle of the highway. With the wind howling and the mixture of rain and sand beating against her, she hadn't even heard the truck approach. By the time Sir Galahad of the gray hair and the granite jaw had loomed up beside her, it was all she could do not to hurl herself into his arms and bawl her eyes out.

Which was so totally out of character she knew she must be even sicker than she'd thought. Every bone in her body ached, including her head. Her throat was so sore she could hardly swallow, and her legs felt about as sturdy as wet linguini. All that on top of a whole mountain range of stress and desperation, and it was no wonder she was irrational. A rational woman would have given up long ago.

He was taking her home with him. She didn't know him from Adam, yet she'd meekly crawled up onto his horse and galloped off into the sunset, bound for heaven only knew where. Or what.

Ru, even more than most people, had reason to be wary of strangers. By tomorrow her sense of survival would probably have resurfaced, but at the moment she was simply too tired, too discouraged and too utterly miserable to care.

They turned off the highway and followed a crooked sand road. Headlights picked out moss-hung live oaks and ghostly dead pines and glints of water. The house, when they finally reached it, was no more inspired than the landscaping. Of the shoebox school of architecture, it sat on a row of naked posts along a low ridge. There was no welcoming light in the window, no smoke from a chimney. The place looked bleak and deserted.

Oh, Lordy, what have I got myself into now?

Ru thought fleetingly of the house where she'd spent half her life. Two sprawling stories of whitewashed brick, set off with magnolias, camellias and banks of azalcas. There was a paved circular drive where Colley, the butler, had taught her to rollerskate and ride a bicycle.

The apartment she'd left the day before yesterday consisted of two furnished rooms, complete with mice and cockroaches. Come to think of it, a shoebox perched on a row of naked pilings looked pretty good, even without a lamp in the window and a roaring fire on the hearth. As long as there was a spare bed inside.

"I'll bring in your suitcase so you can change into dry clothes."

Her suitcase. She had three morc, plus several boxes, a few framed pictures and two file drawers she'd as soon see consigned to the bottom of the ocean. They were all in the trunk of her car.

"Thank you," she rasped, trying to remember what was in her carry-on bag besides shoes. Nothing of value. She'd become so paranoid she wouldn't dream of leaving anything valuable where it could be seen and stolen, which was why she'd crammed all but the smallest bag into the trunk of her car. And forgotten it.

"I'll deal with your car later, but right now we'd better get you into something warm and dry. I'll make us a pot of coffee—I think I might even have a can or two of soup. Bathroom's through there. Help yourself to anything you need.''

She nodded. Even that small exertion was too much. Aspirin, a bed and a dozen blankets, that was what she needed. That and a functioning brain.

''I didn't catch your name.'' Her host glanced at her expectantly.

It didn't matter, Ru told herself. He couldn't be the one. She'd left all that business behind. Once when Ruanna's father, an ardent sports fisherman, had wanted to buy a place out here on the Outer Banks, her mother had described it as the ends of the earth.

The ends of the earth had sounded like Heaven. Or at least a haven.

''It's Ru,'' she said, sounding more like a bullfrog than ever.

''Beg pardon?''

''Ru. Short for Ruanna.'' She'd been named for her two grandmothers, Ruth and Anna, but the less he knew about her, the safer she would feel.

''Ru. Right. Well, Ru, like I said, the bathroom's that way, there's aspirin in the medicine cabinet and plenty of hot water if you want a bath. What I mean is—well, you're bound to be cold, and a hot bath might be the quickest way to warm you up again. I'll heat us some soup.''

She didn't look much better, Trav concluded some twenty minutes later. She was wearing the same clothes, but different shoes. At least her feet and her hair were dry. Her hair, straight, thick and shoulder length, was some smoky color that wasn't exactly brown and wasn't exactly blond. At least she was no longer shivering.

''Find the aspirin?''

"Yes, thanks," she croaked. "Sorry to be such a nuisance."

"No problem," he said as he dished up two bowls of vegetable soup and dug out a tube of saltines. "A bad cold's nothing to sneeze at."

Trav waited as she stared at him for about six seconds, and then she groaned. Either her health had taken a sudden turn for the worse or she had a low tolerance for bad puns.

Over the light supper he had a chance to study her. She was younger than he'd first thought. He'd been right about her eyes, though. They were gray, with a hint of green, like Spanish moss after a rain.

He had a funny feeling those clear eyes of hers weren't quite as transparent as they looked, though. He could read her only up to a point. Enough to know she was hurting. Enough to know she was scared. Enough to know she was hiding something, but as to what it was, he didn't even want to know.

He did know she was wilting fast. Probably used the last of her strength beating the hell out of her old clunker—for all the good it had done.

"By the way, I called the garage. They can't get to your car until morning. Washout just below Frisco has everything south of here blocked, and there's a cut just north of where we left her that's blocking traffic until they can get a road plow in."

"Her?"

"Your, uh—car?"

"Oh. *That* her." She nodded and winced, as if even that small action put a drain on her resources.

"I'm not sure how much you know about the lay of the land, but Frisco's the village just south of where we are now. Hatteras is the next one down the line," he explained. "Technically it's more west than south, but most people think north and south when they picture the Banks."

She nodded again, but he could tell he wasn't getting through. In fact she looked just about ready to fall face first into her soup bowl.

"Ma'am—Ru—why not turn in? They say sleep's the best medicine for a cold. While you're sacked out I'll go retrieve whatever else you need from your car. With my four-wheel-drive, I ought to be able to get through."

While he was at it, he'd clean the thing out in case it didn't make it through the night. It wouldn't be the first time a vehicle had disappeared without a trace.

"Keys in my purse," she said, her voice momentarily improved by the hot soup and coffee. "May I try to call Moselle again?"

"Be my guest." He didn't think much of her chances. Even if she made contact, it wasn't going to do her much good with the road washed out.

She stood and gathered up her bowl and cup, looking lost and helpless. Against every grain of common sense he possessed, Trav found himself wanting to take them out of her hands, wanting to take her in his arms and promise her that everything would be all right. He held back, partly because he was in no position to promise her anything, partly because, like every other serviceman, he'd been trained to avoid anything that could possibly be construed as sexual harassment.

But mostly because the temptation to hold her, to reach out to her, was so strong. He didn't trust his instincts where women were concerned.

He looked her over and reached the conclusion that she was a lot stronger than she looked, despite appearances. There might be shadows under her eyes and a droop to her pale lips, but somewhere underneath that fragile exterior he had a feeling there was a solid core of steel.

"I think you'd better hit the sack, ma'am. I changed the sheets this morning. If you need more covers, look in the locker at the foot of the bed."

Personally, he liked to sleep with the windows open year round. Under the circumstances that might not be a good idea.

For the next two days Trav found himself playing reluctant host to a stubborn, close-mouthed, suspicious woman in a small, bare house with only one finished bedroom and a few mismatched pieces of furniture. It was not a comfortable situation, but he didn't see what choice he had. If his guest had a single social grace, she must have left it hidden under the floormat of her car, which by now was probably buried under a few tons of sand and salt water.

At last report, one tow truck was stuck in the washout south of Frisco, another one had been caught on the wrong side of the S-curve, north of Chicamacomico until the road crews could scrape the highway. And that would take a while because a section of the Oregon Inlet bridge, which had been damaged and rebuilt a few years ago after a barge slammed into it in a storm, was showing signs of sinking again. Heavy equipment was being held back until they could get a ferry up and running.

Life on the Outer Banks wasn't always easy, but of all the places Trav had been stationed in his twenty-year career—Alaska, Hawaii, Connecticut, the U.S. Virgin Islands, not to mention all the places he'd lived as a kid, following his old man—he'd never found one that suited him better.

Mostly the woman, whose full name was Ruanna Roberts according to the registration on her car, slept. It was just as well. Trav had things to do, and he didn't need any more delays.

He stopped by the exchange and picked up extra milk, extra coffee, a few more cans of soup and a supply of aspirin, just in case. While he was out he bought some groceries for Miss Cal, fed her chickens and walked her dog. After listening to her comments, mostly unflattering, about the government, old bones and cable TV, he loaded her porch with firewood and drove home.

Ru was still sleeping, but the coffeepot he'd left half-full was empty and unplugged. Evidently she hadn't slept all day. It felt odd, having someone else in the house. Not necessarily bad, just odd.

Get used to it, Holiday. With any luck at all, you'll be sharing quarters on a permanent basis.

Feeling a familiar tug of emotion, he put through another call, reached Sharon, took a deep, steadying breath and asked to speak to his son.

"Matt's in school."

He'd forgotten the time difference. There was a long silence, and then, "How come whenever I call, he's never available. If it's not school it's soccer practice. If it's not that, he's sleeping over with a friend. Give me a break, Sharon. He's my son, dammit."

"I see you haven't changed. If you don't get your way, you resort to swearing. Maybe it's better if I don't let you meet him at all. I don't think you'd be a very good influence."

"Oh, and I suppose Saint Andrew is a great influence," he jeered. Trav had never even met the man. For all he knew, Andrew Rollins was an ideal role model, but dammit, Matthew was *his* son, not Rollins's. Trav had never even spoken to the boy, much less seen him. He still found it hard to believe that for the past twelve years he'd had a son, and until eleven months ago he hadn't even known about him.

Damned if he wasn't tempted to threaten her again with a lawyer, but if he knew Sharon—and he did, having been married to her for a few miserable years a long time ago—that would only get her back up. As she'd been quick to point out the first time he'd mentioned joint custody, the law would side with her. At the time he'd been a bachelor living in rented rooms, and she was able to provide a home and a stable family. "Three guesses which side social services will come down on," she'd taunted.

Trav had bitten his tongue and reminded himself that she'd been the one to get in touch with him after all this time, to tell him he had a son. She'd hardly have done that if she meant to keep them apart.

Trav had never claimed to be a family man. What he was, was a duty-bound, by-the-books career serviceman. He'd been called a loner. If so, it was only because he didn't know how to be anything else. He was no better at relationships than his own father had been, as Sharon had pointed out more than a few times. But sixteen years ago, head over heels in lust, if not in love, he'd been willing to learn.

Evidently he hadn't learned fast enough or well enough. Now, at the advanced age of thirty-nine, he might not know much about families and forming close ties, but he was determined to give it his best shot. Matthew was his own flesh and blood.

Trav's first impulse on learning that he had a twelve-year-old son was to fly out to the West Coast where Sharon now lived with her second husband, their two daughters and Matthew. But she'd told him to wait. To give her time to prepare the boy for the fact that Andrew Rollins was not his real father.

So he'd waited, and then waited some more. While he was waiting, he'd bought a few acres and started building a house. Next he'd looked around for someone to help him create some semblance of a stable family, to tip the scales in his favor in case it was needed. Meanwhile, he'd sent money and arranged for child support to be taken from his paycheck, and he'd started writing to the boy. He'd sent pictures. He'd sent a baseball glove, soccer gear, a football and a spinning rod, complete with a fully equipped tackle box.

He'd written a bunch of stuff he probably shouldn't have, all about how his own father had been career Coast Guard, and how one of Trav's mother's ancestors had owned thousands of acres in northeast North Carolina, but by the time her descendents had found out about it, it had dwindled to a few hundred acres of swamp that was now part of a wildlife refuge. He'd promised that one day they'd explore it together, canoeing, backpacking—whatever it took.

Oh boy, he'd gone way out on a limb. Trying to establish some kind of a relationship, he'd barged in without waiting to be invited. Being able to size up a situation quickly and act on it was an advantage in his line of work. It could mean the difference between success and failure. But in personal matters it could lead to a situation he didn't know how to handle.

Matthew had never written back, but Sharon had assured him that it was only because he was ashamed of his poor handwriting and was working hard on improving it. She'd said something about one of those learning disabilities that had been discovered recently. A lot of bright kids had it. Some of them even took pills for it.

Things had changed since he was a kid. Trav was just beginning to realize how much he didn't know about being a parent.

After giving up on another fruitless attempt to reach his son, he dialed the number of Ru's friend, Moselle Sawyer, and got the same irritating message. He yawned, then sneezed and then turned as his houseguest shuffled into the living room.

"Someone named Kelli called while you were out. She said she'd call back. I left a note in the kitchen."

"You sound better."

"I've decided to live."

"Glad to hear it." She looked better. In fact, she looked a hell of a lot better, even with her hair in a shaggy braid down her back and a limp black sweater that did nothing at all for her looks.

"Who's Kelli?" She handed him a note she'd written on the back of an envelope.

Trav glanced at the note, then looked over at the woman who'd spent the past forty-eight hours in his bed. The thought that ran through his mind was not only inappropriate, it was impractical. She was a lot better looking than he'd first thought, if a man happened to like his women long, lean and chilly.

Personally, he liked them warm, with a little more meat on the bone. Plus a lot more animation. But then, he'd traveled down that road before and had no intention of repeating the mistake. "She's my fiancée. My ex-fiancée, that is. We're, uh—still on friendly terms."

Kelli was nothing if not friendly. It was one of the things he'd liked best about her—she was always up.

Bright, chipper, talkative. If, after a while it had begun to get on his nerves, he figured that was his problem, not hers. ''Did she say why she was calling?''

''No. She sounded sort of surprised when I answered. She asked if I was Sharon. Who's Sharon?''

Somewhere between boot camp and being commissioned, Trav had picked up a few manners. Hell, he'd even graduated from knife-and-fork class, like every other mustang trying to become an officer and a gentleman.

So he politely refrained from telling her that it was none of her business. ''Sharon is my ex-wife, Ms. Roberts, currently happily remarried and living on the West Coast. Now, is there anything else you'd like to know?''

So much for gentlemanly manners. If he'd tossed a lit firecracker in her lap, she couldn't have looked more startled.

Startled?

Make that frightened.

Two

"Sorry. I didn't mean to be rude, Ms. Roberts."

"How did you know my name?"

He frowned. "Your name?"

"You called me Ms. Roberts. I didn't tell you that."

If there'd been any color at all in her face before, it was gone now, except for the shadows under her eyes. "It's on your registration. Ruanna Roberts? That is you, isn't it?"

The lady was a walking minefield. "Look, I'm sorry. If you're a spook on assignment, or in the witness protection program, I don't want to know about it. It's none of my business. I just thought it might be a good idea to clean out the trunk of your car before it— Anyway, I grabbed the papers from the glove compartment while I was at it, and I happened to see the name."

Her shoulders lifted and fell, making him aware for

the first time that she wasn't quite as skinny as he'd first thought. At least, not all over.

"I'm the one who should apologize. I'm not—not either of those things you mentioned. It's just that—well, I have this thing about privacy," she finished weakly.

"That makes two of us."

"I'm sorry. I'm being silly about this, I know—it's just that I don't really know anything about you, yet you've taken me in and fed me, given me your bed—given me the shirt off your back. Literally." Her voice was still husky, but it no longer sounded quite so painful.

"No big deal. Anyone would've done the same thing." As the bag he'd brought along the first night had held mostly shoes, he'd lent her a pair of his old sweats to sleep in, and because her sweater was still damp, he'd lent her a flannel shirt.

"Maybe not to you. I don't know what I would've done if—" She rolled her eyes. "I talk too much. I always do when I'm uncomfortable. Why don't I just go change your bed and pop the linens and sweats into the washer before I leave? I appreciate all you've done, I really do." She stood up, all five feet six or seven inches of her. All hundred fifteen or so pounds, nicely—if somewhat too sparsely—distributed.

"Don't bother," he said, his gaze following her as she walked away. Her hips swayed, they didn't twitch. It was a subtle distinction, one he didn't normally notice and didn't even know why he was noticing now. "I'll wash 'em next time I get up a load."

Pausing in the doorway, she glanced over her shoulder. "It's the least I can do before I leave."

He shrugged. If she wanted to do his laundry, who

was he to stop her? She wouldn't be going anywhere today, though. Too many bad stretches of road that weren't going to get much better until the scrapers could get down here and uncover any highway that was left under all that sand.

Besides which, her car was a total loss. One of the linesmen had taken a look at it while he was out checking poles. They might be able to use it to help fill up any washout, but that was about all it was good for. He hoped she had insurance on the thing.

She dragged her luggage into the living room, and then she looked at him expectantly. He pretended not to notice. Whether or not she realized it, she was in no condition to go off on her own, even if she had a means of transportation. Whatever bug she'd had had knocked the starch out of her.

This situation was getting pretty dicey. Unfortunately he couldn't come up with a single regulation that covered it. "I've got work to do," he muttered.

"But—"

"Road might be clear by this afternoon. I'll check it out in a couple of hours."

While he laid out another wall of paneling in the room that would be Matt's, Trav tried to come up with a solution. The woman was sick. She was without transportation and Hatteras Island didn't run to streetcars and taxis. The friend she was expecting to visit was currently unavailable, and as for the job…

Dicey situation. About all he could say for it was that it took his mind off the frustration he'd felt ever since he'd learned about his son.

Trav had always considered himself a patient man. He worked hard at cultivating the trait. His father hadn't had the patience to deal with a wife and a son. His cousin Harrison had ended up in the coronary care unit before he'd learned that a man had to accept certain limitations and shape his life around them the best way he could, if he wanted to survive.

He held up another board and reached for his hammer. Working outside on a pair of sawbucks, he'd measured and cut all the paneling to size before the weather closed in. His carpentry skills were on a par with his housekeeping skills. Adequate, with room for improvement.

Most of the work had been contracted, but he'd wanted to do as much as possible with his own hands, not only to save money. There was a lot of satisfaction in building a home for his son with his own hands.

"Do you want coffee?" Ruanna Roberts called out from the kitchen. Evidently she'd given up on waiting for him to offer to drive her wherever she was going.

He should have offered to drive her to the nearest motel or, at least, the nearest one that was open this time of year. Rescuing survivors was second nature to a man with his training. Rescuing, offering shelter. That much he'd done without hesitation, only what now? He had an uneasy feeling the job wasn't done yet.

"Travis? Coffee?"

"Yeah, sure—thanks."

Come to think of it, he could use something hot to drink. His chest ached, probably from trying to sleep on his stomach on the sofa with his feet hanging off the edge. His throat felt kind of dry and scratchy, too, from all this talking. He wasn't used to having company.

She made good coffee. "What's this stuff?" He eyed the plate she set before him suspiciously.

"Sugar toast. Haven't you ever had sugar toast?" The look on his face told Ruanna all she needed to know. He'd never heard of sugar toast. ''If I could've found your cinnamon, it would have been cinnamon toast. You know—butter, sugar and spice?''

''Yeah, sure.''

The way he said it made her think he'd never even heard of cinnamon toast. Not that it was important one way or the other. All the same, she had to wonder what his childhood had been like. Cinnamon toast had been one of her favorite treats as a child. Maybe it was a girl thing.

''It's beginning to clear up,'' she observed. Sooner or later it had to. She'd been here three days and had yet to see the sun.

Of course, she'd slept through the first two days. Whatever had ailed her, it had been no mere cold. Flu, more than likely.

As for the depression she'd been fighting off, she couldn't really blame it on a virus. A person would have to be crazy not to be depressed when, one right after another, like a row of dominoes, her marriage had fallen apart, her family had been rocked by scandal and death, her identity was stolen, her credit rating ruined, her job lost. Let's not forget the crank caller who had insisted on making her life hell. And then, on top of all that, her car had broken down, which forced her to throw herself on the mercy of a stranger.

Being depressed only proved she was sane.

''I'm afraid I've got some bad news for you.''

It was all she could do not to laugh. As if she'd had any other kind of news for the past few years. About the best thing that had happened to her lately was finding the owner of a stray cat that had shown up on her doorstep back in November. The last thing she'd needed was a cat.

But then, after it was gone, she'd cried for half a day. "Bad news? No thanks, I don't care to hear it."

He shrugged. "Your choice. Look, I've got to run out to check on a neighbor. Is there anything you need while I'm out?"

Only my car. Only my friend. Only my job and my life back. "I can't think of a single thing, but thanks. If you'll just give me the name of the garage where you had my car towed, I'll see if it's ready. It was probably only a clogged fuel line. It acted like it was out of gas, but I'm pretty sure..."

Her voice trailed off. She didn't like the way he was looking at her, not quite meeting her eyes. "You're going to tell me it's not a clogged fuel line, aren't you? It's something more serious. Something expensive."

Ru tried to remember how much money she had left after filling up the gas tank. Three twenties. One fifty. A few fives and several ones. It would have to last her until she was working again. She didn't owe anyone anything, thank goodness. She would never trust credit cards again; thankfully, she'd learned to get by on practically nothing.

The car had been a necessity. An expensive one, as it turned out—but she could hardly have walked from Atlanta to the Outer Banks. It had been the cheapest thing on the lot, and the dealer had assured her that aside from peeling vinyl and a few dents, it was basically sound. When she'd asked if he thought it would get her to the Outer Banks, he had assured her that it was just what she needed for a long trip. Plenty of trunk space and a comfortable ride.

"They tried to pull it out," Trav was saying. "Your car? I'm talking about your car." He had an earth-to-Ru look in his eyes, so she stopped silently damning the used-car dealer and mentally counting her money, and tried to look attentive.

"Like I said, they hooked her up and tried to haul her out, but she started coming apart. They tried digging, but you know how quicksand is."

"No, I don't. I'm not interested in learning about quicksand, I just want my car back. In good running condition. There was nothing wrong with it when we left it except that it wasn't running."

He said something about a yellow blob rising above the dunes that didn't register. She stared at his hair. It was cut too short and turning gray. Prematurely, judging from the rest of him. He was weathered, whipcord tough, but he wasn't old. She was still studying his irregular features when his words sunk in.

"That's not possible," she said flatly. "I left it parked on the highway. You were there—you saw where I left it. It couldn't possibly sink right through the pavement."

"Yeah, well—these things have a way of happening. First one wave cuts through the dunes, and then a few more pile in behind it, widening the gap. First thing you know, the road's undermined and whatever happens to be there gets dislodged and starts sinking when the sand traps more water than it can absorb."

"Well, *do* something! Cars can't just disappear!"

"It didn't disappear. Like I said, it's still there, only it's buried up to the rearview mirror. They'll probably bulldoze it out once they start repairing the road. I'm sorry, Ru. I'll be glad to drive you to Manteo to look for a new one once the road's open again. Or you can wait and go with your friend. She might even be able to find you something down here, but I'd have it checked out by a mechanic first. This climate's not too good on cars."

Ru swallowed hard. She wasn't going to cry. She wasn't going to panic. She'd already lost practically everything in the world she had to lose. What was one noisy, smelly, gas-swilling old junker in the grand scheme of things? At least she had her health back.

Trav watched the parade of emotions pass through those rainwater clear eyes of hers. The rims weren't red now, they were only slightly pink. Her nose was no longer red, either. Pretty damned elegant, in fact, as noses went. As were the cheekbones. Sharon would have killed for cheekbones like that.

"You all right?" he ventured, after giving her time to absorb the bad news.

She smiled. Actually smiled. He felt something shift inside him and chalked it up to the sugar toast. He wasn't much for sweets. Now and then he might buy himself a cake or a pie when the ladies had a bake sale, but only to help out the cause. Basically he was a meat-and-potatoes man.

"It looks as if I'll have to ask you for one more favor. Could you possibly drive me to wherever Moselle lives? If she's still not there, I'll camp out on her doorstep until she shows up. I'm pretty sure it's not going to rain anymore."

He wouldn't bet on it. He wouldn't bet on her hooking up with her friend anytime soon, either. With tourist season expanding at both ends, February was about the only month the business community had to take a break.

"What'd you say your friend did at the restaurant? She owns it?"

"Not yet, but she hopes to. Right now she's only the assistant manager."

Before he could comment on that, the phone rang. He happened to be looking at her at the time. She covered it well, but he'd seen panic before. That was pure panic he saw in her eyes before her lids came down and she took a deep breath.

He reached for the phone, never taking his eyes off the woman sitting tensely on the edge of one of his three chairs. "Holiday," he said. "Yeah. Sure, I don't mind. No, it's no trouble. Who? Kelli, what difference does it make? No, it has nothing to do with Matthew. Look, I'll take care of it for you, all right?"

He hung up the phone, waiting for the questions to begin. Women. Were they all like this? Curious as cats, wanting to know everything about a man's private life?

He'd liked to think it was due to jealousy, but any illusions he'd had along those lines had evaporated a long time ago. Before she could be jealous, a woman had to care. The only thing Sharon had ever been jealous of was what other women had that she couldn't afford.

As for Kelli, she was too pretty to be jealous of anyone. His ego had taken more of a beating than he'd expected when she'd dumped him a week before the wedding date. Not that he'd let on. He'd never been one to show his feelings. It had been a mistake right from the first, thinking a wife might make it easier to stake his claim on his son.

He'd told her right up front about Matthew, but he'd told her that wasn't the only reason he wanted to marry her. He liked her. Who wouldn't? She was bright and pretty, popular with everyone who knew her. He couldn't believe she'd even gone out with him, much less agreed to marry him, but she had. He'd just started on the house, and she'd been excited about moving into a brand-new house, although she'd have preferred something bigger, showier—preferably on the beach.

He could still see her, walking around the foundation, going on and on about rosebushes and stuff like that. She'd said she wanted white walls, so he told her he'd paint the paneling he'd already bought. Hell, she'd even picked out the countertop color in the kitchen. He'd figured gray, now he was stuck with pink. *Pink,* of all damn things.

It had been shortly after that, that things had started to slide downhill. Little things, at first. She claimed headaches. His calls went unreturned. There were quarrels about stuff that didn't amount to a hill of beans.

Trav had never kidded himself about his attractiveness to women. When it came to looks, he was your basic, utility model male. He was healthy. He still had all his teeth. He had the standard allotment of features in approximately the right place, but they weren't anything to get excited about.

On the other hand, kids liked him. Dogs liked him. When a date was required for a service-related function, he'd never had trouble rounding one up. He might have two left feet when it came to dancing—he might not be much of a partying man—but he could have learned if that was what Kelli wanted. She should have told him so.

Instead, she'd trumped up a quarrel and accused him of insensitivity. Of not being romantic. Of not being any fun. He would have tried his hand at being all of the above if she'd leveled with him about what she was looking for in a husband. He thought women wanted security in a marriage. Someone who would be there for them when the going got rough. *That* he could have done. He might not be much on frills, but he was good for the long haul.

For the next couple of hours, while Trav measured for window trim, his houseguest stayed holed up in the bedroom. He wondered if she was all right. The news about her car had hit her hard.

But then, that wasn't the only thing bugging her. He'd had time to study her, even more time to think about her odd reactions. Something didn't quite add up. He had the distinct impression she was afraid of something. Or someone. And while he didn't profess to be the world's greatest host, he didn't think she was actually afraid of him.

He nailed up a board and reached for the next one, his mind busy thinking over his options. Did he pry a few answers out of her and try his hand at fixing whatever was wrong? Or did he pretend not to notice the occasional flare of panic in her eyes?

Who was she running from? What was she afraid of? Why had she come down here in the dead of winter, when she obviously wasn't expected?

Not your problem, Holiday, he told himself. You saw your duty and you did it—now back off.

By suppertime Trav had made up his mind to stay out of it. While the casserole—beans and hotdogs, his specialty—heated in the oven and Ru spread his bed with clean linens, he placed a few more calls, trying to track down her absent friend.

In the end he almost wished he hadn't bothered. Then he could have tossed her bags and boxes into the back of the truck, driven her to Hatteras as soon as the road was clear and dropped her off on the woman's doorstep.

Now, his conscience wouldn't let him take the easy way out.

"Um...applesauce? Salad greens?" she said hopefully, watching him remove the pan from the oven and set it on a block of wood on the table.

"Sorry, I should have thought of it. I'm not much on vegetables, but there might be some canned fruit in the pantry. I'll look."

"No, that's all right, this is fine. It looks...tasty."

Yeah, right. He probably shouldn't have added all that hot sauce. Not everyone was blessed with an asbestos palate. She was more the type for rare roast beef and dainty little salads and things poached in wine, with a side order of sugar toast.

It occurred to him that she might prefer music to the tide data at the Frisco pier that was currently playing on the weather radio.

So he got up and switched off the local weather and turned on his favorite country music station. Judging from the carefully blank look on her face, that didn't quite suit her, either.

"You want music or no music? I've got some tapes out in the truck."

"No, thanks, I'm just fine. I tried Moselle's number again, though, and she still doesn't answer. I'm starting to get worried about her."

Speaking of music, it was time to face it. He'd put it off too long as it was. "About your friend...I happened to be talking to a neighbor of hers this afternoon, and she said Miss Sawyer is somewhere in the Bahamas. The neighbor says she'll be back in about three weeks. The restaurant's closed for the next couple of months."

Trav couldn't bring himself to meet her eyes, knowing what he'd see there. Dammit, he didn't want to feel sorry for her. He was the one with the problems. When it came to tough luck, a friend in the Bahamas couldn't compare with a son he'd never even met. Her friend would be back in a few weeks, but as for him, Matt might be grown before they ever managed to get together.

So he kept his eyes on her hands. She had nice hands. Long and slender, with smooth white skin and pretty nails. No polish, no rings. White knuckles, though. That was a bad sign.

"Ru, level with me. Did your friend know you were coming? If she did, she probably left a key with a neighbor, or maybe she left a note telling you how to reach her."

"I—it was going to be a surprise. I sort of…left home in a hurry. I tried to call along the way, but…"

That was about what he'd figured. She must have taken off with no real plan, which pretty much guaranteed disaster. "Let's think this through before we jump to any conclusions."

"Frankly, I don't much feel like thinking."

Frankly, he didn't, either. Besides, he had a feeling no amount of thinking was going to change the basic facts. At the moment she had no place to go and no means of getting there, short of hiring a beach buggy from one of the sports centers. Somehow he couldn't quite see her hitting the road with all her bags and boxes in a four-by-four bristling with rod holders.

Another thing had occurred to him, something he didn't know quite how to approach. Her finances might not be quite as healthy as her classy tweeds and cashmere coat and sweaters indicated. Even in the off season, rooms down here cost more than a few bucks.

Bottom line: he was stuck with her. Or rather, they

were stuck with each other until one of them came up with a solution.

Morosely she forked up three beans and a chunk of wiener. He watched her lips part, showing a set of even white teeth that had probably sent some orthodontist's kid to college.

And then he watched her eyes widen as steam all but came from her ears.

She lunged for the sink at the same time he reached out to open the refrigerator. "Milk's better—fat coats the tastebuds. Water just spreads the fire."

She drank from the carton before he could grab her a glass. And then she lowered the carton, fanned her face, and gulped down some more. "Oh, my heavenly days, that's *incendiary!*" she gasped.

"I forgot."

"Forgot what, the fire extinguisher?" She was breathing heavily though her mouth, her breasts heaving as if she'd been running hard.

"I've been cooking for years, but I guess my repertoire's pretty limited. Are you going to be all right?"

"If I had any lingering germs, they're dead now. Nothing could possibly live in that environment. Don't you even care about your stomach lining?"

"Never gave it much thought. I guess it's pretty well cauterized by now."

"Yes, well…I think I'll have cold cereal, if it's all right."

"Be my guest. There's the pink stuff and some of that kind with brown sugar and nuts. You might as well finish the milk—I'll get more in the morning."

All thought of the missing Moselle and the interred car was forgotten for the moment. She wasn't going anywhere right away, and they both knew it.

"This time I'll take the sofa," she offered, rising to help him rinse the plates and stack them in the dishwasher. That, too, had been Kelli's idea. He never used it. It would take him a week to get up a load.

"Keep the bed," he offered generously. His chest was beginning to feel as if it had been buried under a few tons of wet sand, along with her car. "I don't mind bunking in the living room. Another couple of days and I'll have the spare room finished."

"Don't hurry on my account. I have no intention of abusing your hospitality any longer than I have to."

"You're not abusing anything, there's plenty of room."

He watched her take in the cramped quarters, and it struck him that she was no more impressed with the house he was building than Kelli had been. He'd designed it himself, and been damned proud of it. It was compact and efficient, with no wasted space or exposed pipes. So what if you had to go through the kitchen to get to the bathroom? At least the plumbing was all in one wall.

"Once I finish furnishing the place, it'll look better. The room on the end's going to be an office. The one I'm paneling now is for my boy. I thought maybe twin bunks. Kids like bunks."

"Your boy?"

He hadn't meant to mention Matthew. Didn't particularly want to have to explain the situation to anyone else. Kelli had sounded sympathetic at first. At twenty-five, he'd figured she'd be the perfect age to bridge the gap between a twelve-year-old boy and a thirty-nine-year-old man who'd never spent much time around kids.

"I didn't realize you had children," Ru ventured.

Trav was searching around for a change of subject when Lady Luck beat him to it.

The power went off.

Three

In the sudden darkness, the silence was pronounced. Gradually, small sounds began to emerge. The all-but-inaudible whisper of the gas furnace. A branch brushing against a corner of the house. An acorn striking the roof sounded unnaturally loud. Ru held her breath. Neither of them spoke, waiting to see if the lights would come back on. If they were still off after several minutes, Trav knew that, odds were, it would take a while.

"These things happen," he observed, his quiet baritone sounding husky, almost hoarse. "I'll light a lamp and go switch on the generator. I haven't wired it in yet."

"Oh," Ru replied, just as if she knew what he was talking about.

A little while later they were sipping hot cocoa made from a mix. Ru would have preferred tea. She had an idea Trav would rather have had coffee, but the occasion seemed to call for something out of the ordinary.

With the noise of the generator in the background, they discussed the vagaries of living on the Outer Banks, subject to nature's whims and the limitations inherent on a barrier island. ''Why did you settle here? It's a long way from Oklahoma City.'' Ru had two ways of dealing with stress. She either talked too much or not at all. This was going to be one of those too-much nights.

He sighed as if he didn't want to answer but was too polite to refuse. Which he probably was. Sick or not, she'd learned a lot about Lieutenant Commander Travis Holiday, USCG, retired, in these past few days. Not that he was talkative, because he wasn't, but a remark here, a comment there, had been enough to go on. With nothing else to do but lie around and recuperate, she'd focused on the man because she hadn't wanted to dwell on her own problems.

She did know that he was genuinely kind. And that he was second-generation Coast Guard and had been born in Oklahoma City, which struck her as a strange place for the Coast Guard. But then, she'd never been farther west than Mississippi.

She knew, too, that he had an overdeveloped sense of duty and an underdeveloped ego, which was surprising in anyone, especially a man. Especially a ruggedly attractive man who didn't pay homage to every mirror he passed, the way Hubert had done. Her ex had taken narcissism to new heights.

Travis Holiday seemed totally unaware of his own rugged appeal. Even she, who had sworn off men—she, who had more problems than Godiva had chocolates—had done a double take at the sight of his lean, denim-clad backside bending over a stack of lumber that morning.

He was appealing, all right. She could have sworn, if she'd even thought about it, that she hadn't a viable hormone left in her body. Stress had a way of doing that to a woman.

At least it had done it to her. Mentally and emotionally, if not physically, she'd been curled up in the fetal position for so long she'd stopped thinking of herself as a woman. She was a victim.

Correction. She had been a victim. Past tense. Her divorce had been rough enough, coming on top of the thing with her father. But half the women she knew had gone through at least one divorce.

Unfortunately that had been only the beginning. She'd begun to feel like a centipede, waiting for the other shoe to drop. And then the other one, and then the other one, ad infinitum. Finally, after filling out enough forms to start her own country in order to officially regain her identity—a process that had taken more than two years—she had begun to build herself a new life.

Except for the phone calls. Evidently, crank calls were a common occurrence. As no actual threats had been made, the overworked, understaffed police force hadn't taken her complaint too seriously. So she'd handled it the only way she knew how, by walking away. By that time there'd been nothing left to stay for.

Trav sneezed, and she slid the box of tissues across the coffee table. "Sorry. That's what you get for being a Good Samaritan.

"Allergies," he muttered.

She smiled knowingly. "I don't think so," she said, but before she could add that hoarseness, flushed cheeks and glittery eyes weren't standard allergy symptoms, the phone rang. As an indication of how far she'd come, both literally and figuratively, she hardly even flinched.

Trav reached for it, stretching his long, lean torso so that his shirt parted company with his jeans on one side. Ru stared at the section of naked, exposed flesh. The man wasn't even wearing an undershirt. She knew very well that flu was caused by a virus and not by the weather. All the same, there was such a thing as being too macho.

"Miss Cal?" He cleared his throat. "No, I haven't heard anything yet, I'll let you know as soon as— He's really bugging you, huh? Yeah, I can do that. I'll bring a few sticks of wood and some kerosene while I'm at it, okay? Sure, no trouble—I'll be glad to take him out for you."

Trav hung up the phone, stretched again, liberating the rest of his shirttail, and then turned to Ru. "I've got to go out for a little while, will you be all right?" She was staring at him with that tight-eyed look again. "What?" he prompted.

"Nothing. Nothing at all," she said hurriedly.

"Come on, Ru, something's wrong. Are you afraid of the dark? Afraid to stay here alone? I can cut off the freezer and let you have more lights."

"No, please, you go right ahead with..."

He watched her knuckles whiten again as she got a good grip on her mug. The sixty-watt bulb he allowed himself, in order to leave enough power for the freezer, refrigerator and water pump, didn't put out a whole lot of light, but it was enough to see that she'd crawled back into her cocoon. "Dammit, Ruanna, talk to me. I can't help you if you're going to clam up."

She took a deep breath. He knew something about

control. Hers didn't come easy. ''I'm not afraid of a power failure. I don't need any help. You just go on and do whatever it is you're going to do and don't worry about me. I might just—um, go out and look around while you're gone.''

''Right. It's pitch-dark out there, the wind's blowing a gale, and you want to go sight-seeing. You go right ahead, lady, don't let a little thing like that stop you. But it's only about twenty-eight degrees, so you might want to put on your coat. You're just getting over the flu, remember?''

And then he had to go and spoil his I-know-what's-good-for-you stance by sneezing three times in a row.

Snatching his leather jacket off the back of a kitchen chair, he slammed out the back door. A few minutes later he was back, a coil of rope over one shoulder and a red metal can in one hand. ''Forgot my flashlight,'' he muttered.

Ru sat there after he left until the mug in her hand lost its heat. Then she got up and dumped the contents into the sink. She wasn't going anywhere, and he knew it.

Dammit, just when she thought she had everything under control, it happened again. Evidently she'd been premature with her self-congratulations. The phone rang, and just like Pavlov's dog she reacted. Hearing all over again the soft laughter, the filthy whispered words, the implied threats that weren't actually threats at all. At least, nothing to interest the police when she'd shown them the words she'd copied down verbatim.

And the horrible thing was, it hadn't been a man who'd done it to her, it had been another woman.

She began to pace. Being alone had never bothered her before, but then, she'd never been in quite this situation before. Even the wind seemed as if it were trying to break in and get to her.

If there'd been a TV set in the house, she'd have turned it on. Even a string of commercials was better than having to endure her own company when she was in this edgy frame of mind, yet, without power, she wouldn't even have that distraction.

Tea. At least he had a gas range. She'd give her eyeteeth for a cup of strong Earl Grey. After rummaging through his kitchen cabinets and finding most of them bare—which struck her as somehow sad—she settled for instant coffee, which she detested. Cup in hand, she returned to the sparsely furnished living room and began perusing the service green metal bookcase.

Her host's taste in literature ran mostly to technical references. *The Coast Guardsman's Manual, U.S. Coast Guard Regulations,* and something called the *U.S. Code Title 15,* none of which sounded terribly exciting. Aside from that, there were several books on radio communications, a trade paperback on German U-boats off the mid-Atlantic in World War II, and—finally—the only work of fiction. An early Asimov anthology.

Unfortunately Ru had never cultivated a taste for science fiction. Flying saucers passed right over her head.

The pun came unbidden, and she groaned. Hubert had taken pains to inform her that puns were the lowest form of humor. She'd reacted by buying a book of the things and lacing her conversations with them. Theirs had not been a marriage made in heaven.

She eased the thick Asimov off the shelf—anything to distract her—and then she remembered the book she'd been reading when she'd decided on the spur of the moment to relocate. Had she tossed it or packed it?

Packed it. By the time her possessions had been

thinned out to where a six-dollar paperback represented a major investment, she'd been into suspense, as if solving someone else's problems would put her own life in order.

"If I were a paperback thriller, where would I be?" she muttered, rummaging in one box after another.

The book had been on her bedside table back in Lawrenceville, and she'd scooped it off and dumped it in with…

Closing her eyes, she visualized. Summer nightgowns, curling brush, her collection of spare purses…

Bingo.

Some women collected shoes. Ru collected handbags. Back when she could afford them, she'd indulged herself with the kind that lasted for years. Naturally that particular box was on the bottom of the stack, under her linens, her summer clothes, the contents of her medicine chest and—

A-ha! Right where she'd tossed it, on top of a beaded evening bag she hadn't used in years and probably never would again. Now all she had to do was to recall who had done what to whom, and why nobody knew it.

Opening the book at random, she skimmed a few pages, trying to pick up the thread of plot. Wandering back to the living room, she tilted the lampshade to wring all the light possible from the small bulb, found the page where she'd left off—marked by a cash register receipt from the bookstore—and read a few more lines.

> The old woman had lived alone. Lived, that is, until someone struck her on the back of the head with a frozen leg of lamb. By the time the body

was discovered, the lamb had thawed and had been half devoured by a pack of feral dogs that had lately terrorized the rural area. Another few hours, and—

"Oh, for heaven's sake," she muttered, and slammed the book shut. If she didn't know better she would have sworn her whole life had been scripted by a cosmic comedian.

To think she'd once possessed a functioning brain. There'd been a time, shortly after she'd walked out on her marriage, when she'd launched on an ambitious plan to reinvent herself. Acting purely on impulse, she had decided to become a paralegal.

Like most of her other impulses, that one had been a mistake. Ultimately she'd faced the fact that even if she managed to get through the correspondence course, it would be far too late to do her any good when it came to negotiating a divorce settlement.

The settlement had been a joke. Her own lawyer, recommended by Hubert's secretary, DeeDee, had gone down without a whimper.

"Sorry," DeeDee had said after the hearing. "She did a real good job for a friend of mine."

Ru had considered DeeDee a friend, too, even if she did have the misfortune to work for that jerk. Furious and broke, Ru had dropped the paralegal course to concentrate on her dual career of waiting tables at a franchise steak house and potting plants for a wholesale nursery. She'd turned to fiction for escape instead of textbooks, starting with what was euphemistically called literature. The only trouble was that most of it was so grim and relentlessly depressing, she'd stopped reading at all. Instead, she'd watched mind-numbing sitcoms. The last thing she needed was more depression.

About the time she'd reached saturation point with giggles, slapstick and silly double entendres, she happened to pick up a paperback romance. It was there she discovered that other people, women not unlike herself, had problems, too. And that they managed to solve them and find true, lasting happiness in the end. It had given her hope.

Lord knows, she'd needed hope. She'd even managed to regain her sense of humor, which Hubert had deplored. When she'd cracked a pun and the whole kitchen staff at the restaurant had broken up, she'd thought she was truly on the road to recovery.

It was then that the curtain had risen on act two of *The Perils of Pauline*. Or in her particular case, *The Ruination of Ruanna.*

Once she'd realized what was happening, she'd been far too busy filling out incomprehensible forms, making frustrating phone calls to bored bureaucrats who'd heard it all before, to read much of anything. Too busy trying to convince her bank, both her employers and all the creditors circling around like vultures over fresh roadkill that there were two Ruanna Robertses—she had taken back her maiden name after the divorce—and that she was *not* the Ruanna Roberts who had maxed out her credit cards, collected a whole slew of traffic tickets and gone through the mall passing bad checks so fast the automated check-checker hadn't been able to catch it.

In desperation, she'd turned to her ex-husband. He was a lawyer, after all. His business was advising people in trouble.

She'd had to go through DeeDee, who screened all

Hubert's calls. Hubert had been less than sympathetic. In fact, she hadn't even been able to speak to him personally, but had had to relay the whole messy affair through DeeDee, a frustrating exercise in futility.

"Mr. Wylie is in conference, Ms. Roberts. He said if you'll call back this afternoon, he'll be glad to recommend a counselor."

"A counselor? As in another lawyer?" She'd been married to the jerk for seven years, and he couldn't even spare her five minutes?

"Gee, Ru, I'm not sure—he might have been talking about a financial counselor, or maybe a psychiatrist."

She'd have stiffed him for the fee, and he knew it. He'd been getting two-fifty to four hundred an hour, depending on the client, when she'd left him. By now, he was probably charging five.

That was when she'd given up on romances and started reading suspense and true crime. If she was going to have to do her own police work, she needed to know how it was done. Evidently she was no good at happy endings, but if other women could solve mysteries, then so could she. She wasn't stupid, only scared and sick and broke and—

God, she hated self-pity. Even when things were about as bad as they could be, she had refused to whine. She'd been mad as the devil, especially when the officer she'd reported the phone calls to hadn't even bothered to glance up from his messy desk.

But she hadn't whined. And she wasn't going to whine now. What she was going to do was coolly evaluate her situation and take the appropriate action. What she was going to do was stop jumping every time the phone rang, and stop reading the wrong meaning into such simple phrases. Trav had said he'd "Take him out

for you.'' If there was one thing she knew about
Holiday, it was that he was no hit man. A rope, a c
phrase and a can of kerosene did not constitute a threat of murder. There was a perfectly logical explanation. Clotheslines. Kerosene heaters.

Meanwhile, she was going to change her reading material. If she read anything at all, it would be cookbooks. Once, in a fit of frustration, she'd baked nine dozen peanut-butter cookies and eaten every one in less than three days. She still couldn't look at a jar of peanut butter without getting queazy.

Pulling a cashmere cardigan from her earlier life more tightly around her, she concentrated on her book, reading without a smidge of comprehension while she waited for…

What?

When she heard Trav's heavy footsteps on the front deck, she laid down her book with a sense of relief. He always stomped the sand off his boots outside— which didn't keep him from tracking the stuff in.

He came in sneezing. Between sneezes, he muttered something about long hair and fleas, tossed his jacket at a chair, slung the rope over a doorknob and raked his fingers through his short brindle hair. ''Is that coffee you're drinking? I can't even smell it, but it looks good.''

''Instant. I can make a pot, though, if you can hook up the coffeemaker to your generator.''

''Instant's fine, but first I need to shower off some livestock.''

Of course he did. Ru hadn't the slightest idea what he was talking about, but she did know he was coming down with whatever she'd had for the past couple of days. Flu—a bad cold—some mutant combination of viruses that struck when a body's defenses were at their lowest ebb.

She had no idea what condition Trav's immune system was in. He struck her as a man with impregnable defenses, the low-profile type who never bit off more than he could chew, never spent more than he could afford and never allowed himself to get too comfortable, knowing that life had a way of sneaking up on your blind side and knocking you for a loop.

Once or twice, though, she'd caught a glimpse of something in his eyes that looked almost like vulnerability. He'd covered it so quickly, that she thought she must have imagined it.

Just as she was stirring coffee crystals into a mug, he emerged from the bathroom, barefoot, wearing a fresh pair of jeans and an open black flannel shirt. Still no undershirt. "What was bugging you before I left?" he asked, leading the way into the living room with his coffee and a jar of salted peanuts. He held out the jar, and Ru shook her head.

"No, thanks."

"They're good for you. I read that somewhere. Ru, you were pretty spooked when I left here. What was that all about? Is it the dark, or being here alone?"

Ordinarily Trav wouldn't have pressed, but something about the woman got to him. He wanted to put it down to the bug that had wiped her out, but it could be she was just naturally flaky.

"I wasn't 'spooked,' as you call it. You're coming down with something—you look feverish to me. That's why you're imagining things."

He shrugged. "If you say so. But any time you feel like talking, I'm a pretty good listener." He didn't know why he was being so persistent. If it was her friend she was worrying about, he couldn't help her. The most he could do was offer to drive her to a motel and leave her there, but without transportation of her own, she'd be stuck.

Besides, he wasn't too sure she could afford it. Her clothes, what few he'd seen, looked expensive, but there was that old car she'd been driving. Something didn't add up.

He was about to make his excuses and say good-night when she surprised him. "You'll laugh if I tell you."

It took him a minute to reconnect. "I won't laugh." The last thing he felt like doing was laughing. "Go ahead. Shoot." He propped one foot on the coffee table, wanting nothing more than to close his eyes and drop out for the next twenty-four hours or so.

Instead, he waited, his gritty eyes never leaving her face. He saw the corners of her mouth twitch, and it struck him that hers was a mouth made for laughter. He had a feeling it hadn't had much exercise lately.

"There you go again," she said. Her voice was recovering from the huskiness that had marked it at first, but it was still soft. "First you're going to take someone out, using a rope and a can of kerosene, now you're talking about shooting. Is it any wonder I was skittish?"

"Skittish. Is that what you call it? From where I stood, it looked like you were scared clean out of your gourd."

She gave a funny little laugh that was more of a hiccough and said, "Blame it on the books I read. Certain phrases have certain meanings in the genre of crime and suspense."

"That's crazy. I read science fiction, but that doesn't mean everytime a transformer arcs I expect a spaceship to land in the middle of Highway 12."

From somewhere Trav remembered reading that the eyes were the window of the soul. He didn't know much about the soul, but he had a hunch her eyes were the window on her mind. Propping the other foot on the table, he leaned back, laced his hands across his belly and watched the thoughts chase across her face like cloud shadows on the beach. Doubt. Indecision. Determination. He knew the exact moment she made up her mind to trust him.

She sighed. "I had a few problems back in Atlanta. At least, it started out in Atlanta, only I didn't realize it at the time."

She fell silent. He waited. Sooner or later she might begin to make sense. So far, she hadn't. He wondered idly if her hair was as soft as it looked, then wondered if it was too soon after his last dose to take a few more aspirin.

"Well, first there was the divorce. I don't suppose any divorce is pleasant."

Silence again. He primed the pump, wanting to get it over with so he could turn in. "Mine wasn't, but you get over it."

Her face instantly registered concern. "Did she take you to the cleaners? No, forget I asked, it's none of my business."

She was right. It wasn't. They'd split everything evenly, which hadn't been a whole lot at the time, but he'd paid alimony until Sharon remarried. He'd never begrudged her anything until he found out he had a son, and that she'd kept it from him all these years.

Thank God they'd been on opposite sides of the country at the time. "We're talking about you, not me," he reminded her.

"Oh. Well…luckily we didn't have children. Maybe

if we had, it might have been different. No, that's not true. I might have stuck it out longer, though."

"Yeah, I know what you mean." If he'd known about Matthew, things would've been different between him and Sharon, but neither of them had known at the time. And for reasons he would never understand, she had chosen not to tell him later.

Ru started to say something. His head was floating, while his body felt as if it weighed a ton. "Look, can this wait until tomorrow? Right now, I'm bushed." He started to cough, slapped a hand over his throat, and swore when he was able to catch his breath.

"Go to bed, Travis. Your own bed, not the sofa. I'll bring you something in a few minutes, if I can find which box I dumped my medicine cabinet into."

Sometime during the night, the power came back on. Looking dreadful, Trav emerged from his room buttoning on a shirt and went outside to do whatever needed doing to the generator. He ignored Ru's offer of help. When he came back inside, he refused her offer of hot milk and cold tablets, and disappeared into his bedroom again.

For the next twenty-four hours, which seemed to be the duration of the curse she'd brought down on him, he slept, waking only to go to the bathroom, drink the hot soup and fruit juice she brought him, and mutter about all the things he needed to do.

Taking his calls because she was getting over her phonophobia—and besides, there was no one else to do it—Ru learned what a few of those things were. He was supposed to deliver meals to shut-ins one day a week. When she explained that he was sick with flu, the person on the other end of the line asked if she could do it instead.

"I'm sorry, but my car's out of service and I don't know my way around yet. I've only been here a few days." True, she'd come here with every intention of staying, at least until she sorted out what she wanted to do with the rest of her life, but she wasn't ready yet to get involved in community affairs.

The next two calls were from California. Miss California, that was. Something about snakes in the sky. "You tell that boy I said if them snakes falls down on my head, sky's going to go crazy."

"Yes, ma'am, I'll be sure and tell him exactly what you said." And she'd thought *her* calls were weird.

"Give him whisky and molasses. Not strong enough so he'll take drunk, just enough to thin out the germs."

Ru promised she would mix up the proper dosage and see that Trav got it as soon as he woke up. "I'll tell him you called, Miss...um, California."

"You tell him about sky and them snakes, and tell him to get on over here as soon as he can. He's a good boy. You going to marry him and take on that son of his? If I weren't rising up on middle age, I might even marry him myself."

Shaking her head slowly, Ru hung up the phone. Without mentioning names, somebody around here was nutty as a fruitcake.

Ru gauged it just right. From the surly way Trav had reacted the last time she'd taken him his medicine, she thought he must be coming out of it. When she heard the shower running, she was sure of it. She gave him time to shave, then started the bacon and coffee and turned up the heat under the hash browns. If she was any judge of men—which, admittedly, she wasn't—he'd come looking for food most anytime now, and not be able to eat half of what he thought he wanted.

Trav paused in the kitchen door, eyes narrowed suspiciously. "What's all this?" he growled.

"I thought you might be hungry."

He scowled, unwilling to give an inch. "I didn't know you could cook."

"There's a lot you don't know about me. I once cooked a complete Thanksgiving dinner for twenty-four people," she admitted modestly. "Hardly anyone got sick."

"Sorry. I guess my manners are still kind of raw."

"Never mind, just sit down and start on it before the toast gets tough and the eggs get cold. You need to get your strength back. I made a list of your calls, and I have a few questions that need answering. Do you want to eat first or talk first?"

Four

The questions could wait. Trav found he was starved. He had the constitution of an ox, but two days without solid food was just about his limit. On the rare occasions when he came down with a cold, he generally ignored it. With anything flulike, he rode it out, then got up, showered and got back to work.

After Sharon had left him, he'd learned to keep a good supply of canned ravioli, Beenie-Weenie and spiced peaches on hand, in case of emergency.

Ru waited until he'd eaten half of what she'd put on his plate before getting out the list that had lengthened as the calls continued to come in. At this rate she might try for an office job. Her computer skills weren't up to speed, but at least the sound of a ringing phone no longer sent her into a tizzy. "The first call was about delivering meals to shut-ins."

"What day is today?"

She told him, and he said, ''Oh, hell, I forgot. I'll do double next week.''

''Fine. Next you had a call from the benevolent order of something or other, wanting you to buy some jelly. I told the man to call back next week, and promised that if you were still among the living you'd order a truckload.''

He reared back and gave her a squinty-eyed glare.

''Just kidding. I told him you were desperately ill, and probably wouldn't be needing any. The next three calls were from Miss California. Travis, is she, um—all right?''

Crossing his arms over his chest, he replied, ''Hundred percent. You just have to take her on her own terms. What'd she want this time?''

''I'm not sure. It sounded like snakes in the sky, and if they fall on her head, something or other will happen. I suppose that makes sense to you, but…well, I thought she might be—well, you know. Anyway, she kept calling, wanting to know how you were. She told me to stir molasses into whisky and give you some every now and again, but not enough so that you'd 'take drunk.' ''

Tipping back his chair, Trav started to laugh. It hurt. His throat was still raw. His chest felt as if it had been filled with concrete and emptied out again, but he was over the hump. ''I guess I'd better start at the beginning. Want me to top off your cup for you?'' He stood to pour himself a third cup of coffee, adding two heaping spoons of sugar.

While Ru scraped plates, rinsed them and stacked them in the washer, he explained about Skye, the Australian sheepdog that had been born deaf due to a genetic flaw. ''Smart as a whip, but he needs more exercise than Miss Cal's able to give him. I've been taking him out for a good workout once or twice a day."

"You 'took him out.' And I guess that explains the rope?"

He nodded. "Trouble is, once he slips his mooring, it's hard as hell rounding him up again. He can't hear calls or whistles. This time of year I usually put him on a long lead and run him up and down the highway. He likes to swim, too, but that'll have to wait another few months."

"You were running up and down the highway? Wearing yourself out in this kind of weather? No wonder you staggered through the door and collapsed."

Oh, for heaven's sake, she'd embarrassed the man. It was none of her business if he wanted to kill himself, only she wasn't used to stoics. Hubert could get more mileage out of a hangnail than any of the professional hypochondriacs he paraded before the bench wearing neckbraces.

"I didn't collapse, I took a nap," Trav informed her.

"Sure you did, Mr. Van Winkle."

His crooked grin was reluctant, but nonetheless effective. "Look, could we please get off my case? What else did Miss Cal have to say?"

"I told you about the snakes. Could I have misunderstood her? I thought snakes were supposed to hibernate in the wintertime."

"Here on the Banks they just sort of doze." He rose and put away the butter and strawberry jam, took her arm and steered her out of the kitchen. "You're not here to work, Ms. Roberts."

"It's hardly work. Besides, it's my fault you got sick. You did me a favor and I repaid it by passing on my bug."

"After this meal, consider us even. Besides, if you want to know the truth, before you came along I was starting to talk to myself. They tell me that's not a good sign in a man my age."

She gave him a skeptical look, and Trav wondered which comment she was challenging, the one about his age or the one about his state of mind. The truth was, he liked living alone. He was used to it. But if he told her that, she might take it the wrong way and get her feelings hurt, and he'd sooner poke his finger in a live socket than hurt her feelings.

"You asked me about Splotch and his friends," he reminded her.

She turned to stare up at him. "I did?"

She was close enough that he caught a whiff of some subtle scent that reminded him of...Christmas?

Evidently a few of his senses weren't back on line yet. "Snakes," he said.

Ru claimed the captain's chair. He took the sofa, aware that his few pieces of furniture looked pretty shabby. He'd picked them up secondhand, thinking there'd be plenty of time later to make changes, when he wasn't so strapped for cash.

She crossed her legs at the ankles and folded her hands gracefully in her lap. He propped his feet on the coffee table, a bad habit he was going to have to overcome. He'd slipped into a few of those, living alone.

She had great ankles, he'd noticed that about her. Come to think of it, she had great everything. He put his interest down to a lingering side effect of the virus. One of the more bizarre symptoms. She smelled like Christmas, looked like one of those skinny fashion models, and reminded him, for some crazy reason, of a grandmother he hadn't thought about in years.

The last time he'd seen Grandma Becky had been the Christmas after he'd started school. His father had been pulling weather patrol in the North Atlantic. For a change, his mother had been on the wagon, so they'd packed up and gone to visit her mother on a farm in the middle of nowhere.

Looking back, he wished he'd spent more time listening to the two of them talk and less wandering around the hot, cluttered room, wondering how soon he could escape outside.

Once his grandmother had caught him tossing one of the dried, clove-studded oranges she kept in a bowl on the mantel, catching it with all the flair of a six-year-old major leaguer. When she'd offered him one, he'd refused. Politely, he hoped. She'd insisted, telling him to put it in his sock drawer, and he remembered wondering if the sock fairy would leave him fifty cents, the way the tooth fairy did when he lost a tooth and put it under his pillow.

All that had been a lifetime ago. He wondered what had ever happened to that old photograph album she'd tried to interest him in. He'd been far more taken by the rusty machinery in one of the unused outbuildings.

God, what a shallow, selfish jerk he'd been. Or maybe just young. At least Matt had a variety of interests. Sports. Sharon said he was pretty good at sports. Trav had never had time for them as a child, or maybe it was because they'd never stayed in one place long enough to get seriously involved. But there were all kinds of wholesome outdoor activities they could share here, and—

Reluctantly, Trav came back to the present to find Ru staring at him expectantly. "Sorry, you were saying—"

"Snakes. She kept talking about snakes."

He cleared his throat and tried to ignore the lingering trace of rawness. "Yeah, well...Miss Cal had a bad case of mice. Her fingers don't work too well in damp weather, which is about the only kind we have down here, so traps aren't practical. She doesn't like having poison around on account of the dog, so I got her a rat snake."

"You got her a *what?*"

"Now, don't go off half-cocked. They're perfectly harmless. You get yourself a good resident rat snake, you won't ever have to worry about mice anymore."

Slowly Ru shook her head. "I don't believe you. You're making this up."

"Coastie's honor. When you move around a lot, living in all kinds of housing, you pick up a few survival tricks. Now, if it's cockroaches you've got, you want yourself a good lizard, but for rats or mice, you can't beat a full-grown rat snake."

"How big is full grown?" Judging from the skeptical look on her face, she still thought he was putting her on.

"Oh, maybe four, five feet."

"I don't believe a word of this, you know. You're good, but I've been conned by experts."

"Yeah, well...that's up to you. You can come with me if you want to. Sounds like Splotch brought home some friends and they're having a party up in Miss Cal's attic. Guess I'd better go check it out."

"Why do you keep calling him—it...whatever—Splotch?" She flung out her hands in that expressive way she had.

Trav wished he weren't feeling quite so washed out. Two days in bed on liquid rations took more out of a man than an egg and a couple of strips of bacon could put back. "Well, you see, snakes are clean—they're about as clean a pet as you'd want. Trouble is, they're hard to housebreak."

The sound she uttered expressed roughly equal parts of disgust and disbelief, so he hastened to explain that as snakes didn't eat too frequently, that wasn't usually a major problem.

Flinging herself out of the chair, Ru began to pace. His quarters weren't what you might call spacious, which tended to cramp her style. Despite feeling like something that washed up on the shore at high tide, Trav couldn't help but admire the way she moved. She was a little too pale, a little too skinny for his taste, but there was something special about her, all the same. Even with a tweed skirt flapping midway down her legs and wearing a couple of layers of baggy sweater, she was well worth watching.

Hours later neither one of them was aware of much beyond the dripping noses, numb feet and the cold northeast wind whipping in off the sound. Shivering and laughing, they stomped the sand off their shoes and hurried inside to the welcoming warmth. For the first time Ru realized that the whole house smelled of raw wood from the unfinished paneling.

"If anyone had told me a week ago that I'd spend hours relocating a family of snakes and more hours chasing a shaggy mutt through the swamp, hauling him bodily from a creek and hanging on to him while he got a bath and a rubdown, I'd have threatened to call the butterfly brigade."

"Consider it your good deed of the day."

"The day? How about the year? I can't believe I actually held a snake in my hands. As much as I like to garden, just touching an earthworm makes my skin crawl.''

''I know what you mean. I like to ride, but touching a horse makes my skin gallop.''

It took a moment, and then she shook her head. ''You're bad. You're even worse than I am.''

He grinned that lopsided grin again, the one that made his eyes gleam like shards of cobalt glass. ''I don't reckon you've ever cleaned a fish, have you?''

''Not personally. Why?'' she asked warily.

''Just wondered if it made your head swim.''

She rolled her eyes, and they both laughed as Trav helped her out of her coat, his hands lingering on her shoulders a few seconds longer than necessary. She discovered in that moment that even cold hands could generate warmth.

Stepping away, she busied herself brushing leaves and twigs from her hair. ''All the same, snakes—! I still don't believe I touched one.''

''Look at it from the snakes' point of view. You think they enjoy being rousted out of a nice warm attic and dumped into an unheated shed?''

''Oh, Lordy, is that going to be a problem? Not for the snakes, for Miss Cal. Does she still use the shed?''

''I wouldn't worry about it.'' Trav shed his own coat. He'd lent her a pair of his jeans and a flannel shirt, both of which were now wet and muddy. She had briar scratches on her hands and a collection of dried weeds on various parts of her body that were starting to itch. ''Once the weather warms up so she can get around better, Miss Cal'll be able to deal with just about anything that comes along. She's a pretty sharp lady.''

''She likes you, too. She said she'd marry you and

help look after your son if she weren't rising on middle age.''

Actually, Miss Cal had asked if Ru intended to marry him and help look after his son.

''Yeah, well...I guess you might call her middle-aged if you figure old age at about a hundred and forty years.''

She hung both coats in the utility room to dry. Her cheeks burned. Her nose was frozen and would probably drip once it thawed. She must look awful, but she couldn't remember feeling so alive. ''I've never done anything even faintly like this, not even as a child.''

''Deprived childhood, huh?''

''Great childhood, but no pets. Mama said they spread disease.''

Trav nudged the thermostat. He looked ruddy. Weathered. An outdoor man in his natural element. He even smelled like outdoors. She found herself wanting to bury her nose in his throat and inhale, only first she'd better find a tissue and blow.

He watched her with a look that was oddly intent. A look that made her suddenly self-conscious. She mumbled something about a handkerchief and a hot bath and turned away, the wet legs of his jeans flapping against her ankles.

''Good idea.'' Trav stared after her, her words eliciting a subliminal glimpse of the two of them sharing a bath. Every male hormone in his body endorsed the idea enthusiastically, and he told himself that the sooner her friend got back, the better off they'd both be. He wasn't entirely sure yet just what Ru's problem was, but he had his own course all mapped out, and it didn't include getting involved with a woman.

''This mud stinks to high heavens,'' she called

through his bedroom door. They hadn't yet settled the matter of who slept where, but her clothes were still there.

"You didn't have to dive into the creek, you know," he called back. "I had him cornered."

He was still standing there when the door opened and Ru emerged, wearing a quilted satin bathrobe and a pair of his hunting socks. There was a spatter of mud on her forehead. "You had him cornered, all right," she scoffed. "I saw the crazy mutt ram into the back of your legs and knock you down."

Without thinking, he reached out and tucked a damp curl behind her ear. He'd never been much of a toucher. Evidently his hands had a mind of their own. "Herding instinct," he said gruffly. "We were too far apart and he was trying to get us back together."

"Yes, well, if I hadn't waded in after you, the big clown would have knocked you down and sat on you. I tried yelling at him, but it didn't work."

Trav had to laugh, but the laughter quickly turned into a cough. Ru sneezed. She said, "I have a feeling we might both regret the day's work, but I have to admit, it was fun while it lasted, wasn't it?"

He nodded, his eyes never leaving her face. "Know something else? For a lady who wears cashmere and handwoven tweeds, and speaks with a silver-spoon accent, you're a pretty good sport."

"What do you mean, pretty good? I'm a damn good sport."

He leaned forward until his forehead touched hers. "Yep," he said, his voice gravelly and laden with meaning neither of them cared to explore too deeply. Moving away, he took a deep breath. "I think this calls for hot coffee with a shot of Jack Daniel's."

"Or hot tea, with extra-strength cold tablets, if we have any left." She looked bemused, slightly bewildered.

Or maybe he was the one who was bewildered. Something had sure as hell shorted out his circuits. "We could always try Miss Cal's remedy."

"Whisky and molasses? Count me out," she said with a breathless little laugh.

Trav couldn't help himself. He caught her by the shoulders and gave her a gentle shake. Teasing. Just playing around. The only trouble was, it didn't feel like playing, it felt like something else. Something he wasn't used to, wasn't looking for and sure as hell didn't need. His life was complicated enough, as it was.

"Go on, get your bath before you get sick again. I'll make fresh coffee."

"One of us needs a bath, all right. I'm not mentioning any names here, but *somebody* stinks to high heaven."

In a more unenlightened age, he might have swatted her playfully on the bottom. Instead, he growled, "Quit complaining, woman, it just proves your nose is back in working order."

After she shut the bathroom door, he stood there for several minutes, listening to the small, intimate sounds on the other side of the door. Picturing her stepping into his tub, ducking her head under his shower, reaching for his soap.

"Don't be a fool, Holiday," he warned softly. Still in his muddy clothes, he poured himself a cup of old coffee, laced it with whiskey, refilled the pot and headed for the living room. Then he reached for the phone.

Some twenty minutes later he sat back, propped his sock feet on the table, then thought better of it and set them back onto the floor. Sooner or later he was going to have to pick out a few decent pieces of furniture. Maybe he'd get an easy chair when he went shopping for Matt's bunk beds. What kind of furniture, he wondered, did Ru like?

Antiques, probably. The kind of stuff that had been in the family for generations. Big oil paintings with heavy gold frames. Lots of carved crystal sitting around on polished mahogany. Good thing she wouldn't be around much longer, or he might slip up and ask her to help him pick out a few things before Matt came to stay. He wanted the place to be perfect when the boy first walked in. Not too stuffy—not too cluttered, the way his grandmother's house had been, but like a home ought to look. The kind of home where two guys could be comfortable together.

If he asked her for a few pointers, she might feel obligated to pay for her room and board by staying to help him out. All other considerations aside, the last thing he wanted was her gratitude.

Oh, yeah? And what's the first thing, Holiday?

Funny how quickly a guy could get used to having someone else around. Living in base housing, he was used to being around people, but he'd always valued his privacy. Sharon had called him a loner.

Kelli had called him a selfish, old stick-in-the-mud who'd forgotten how to have a good time, if he'd ever learned.

He wasn't at all sure he had, come to think of it.

Yeah...he knew how to have a good time. He'd had one today. With Ru. With Ru and that clown of a dog. So maybe he wasn't good at relationships, but he could learn.

He was damned well going to learn, because the older he got, the more he realized what he'd been missing out on all these years. Sharon had promised to send Matt to him for the summer, and he was going to hold her to it. He might just fly out there and bring the boy back with him.

Matthew Holiday. He'd have to see about having his name legally changed. She'd let him grow up thinking he was Rollins's son, but all that had changed now. Trav didn't even know what the kid looked like. With any luck he'd inherited his mother's features, preferably without her vanity.

His own parents had blue eyes. Both he and his old man had dark hair. He had no idea what color his mother's original hair color had been. More often than not, it had been some shade of red or reddish blond.

Trav wondered if the local school fielded a soccer team. Half the time when he called, Matt was off at soccer practice. He would find out what was available on the island. Meanwhile, he'd see if he could squeeze the price of a boat into his budget. He'd shelled out a lot for land and construction costs, but he still had a few bonds he could cash.

Fishing. A father-son sport if there ever was one. If the kid was competitive, there were tournaments.

Later on, maybe he could swing a recommendation to the academy. On the other hand, there was something to be said for coming up through the ranks, the way he had. Mustangs were a special breed.

Either way, three generations of Coast Guard wouldn't be a bad heritage to pass along.

Heritage…

"Travis? Trav, wake up."

"Whaaa…"

"You were sleeping with your mouth open. It'll

make your throat sore again, and besides, you still haven't changed out of your wet clothes."

"Yes, ma'am. No, ma'am."

Ru thought he looked flushed, even feverish. You'd think any man who had achieved the rank of lieutenant commander would have sense enough to take care of his health. "Is your throat sore again?"

He gave her a sheepish look.

"I thought so. You march right into that bathroom, take off your clothes and climb into that bathtub. There's plenty of hot water left."

Trav started to make some fresh remark about bossy women, but before he could finish it he broke into a hacking cough. Ru didn't know whether to hug him or swat him. Wanting to do both, she did neither. "Go on, I'm going to mix up some of Miss Cal's cough syrup and if I can borrow your truck, I'll go see what the pharmacist has in the way of over-the-counter cold remedies. We've used up all mine."

"Keys're in my pants pocket."

"Hand them over."

"Come get 'em," he dared her. He was doing his best to be outrageous, but it wasn't working. He was obviously on the verge of a relapse. His voice sounded like a rusty hinge.

Ru waited until she heard splashing from the bathroom, then put on her coat and let herself out. It had been years since she'd driven a stick shift, but fortunately, traffic was light. She remembered seeing a sign that said pharmacy, but couldn't remember how far it was. All she'd seen of Buxton was the highway they'd come in on, so it couldn't be that hard to find.

While she was there she could ask about a grocery store. She might as well stock up on soup makings and tea, and whatever else she could think of to tide them over until she could make other arrangements.

It took her a while to track down the pharmacy. It took slightly longer to recognize the fact that the woman who was tooling down the highway in a borrowed pickup truck bore no resemblance whatsoever to the poor wimp who'd crept out of Lawrenceville, Georgia, no more than a week ago.

Ru didn't recall too much about the last leg of her trip; her head had been on a fever trip of its own. She did remember seeing water on both sides of the highway, feeling miserable, frightened and desperately alone. By the time her car had died, she'd been wondering what in the world had possessed her to jump off the edge of the earth without a net.

And then along came a grizzled knight in unshining armor, riding to the rescue in a rusty silver pickup truck.

She'd had no choice but to go with him. By the time she could think clearly again, he'd been coming down with whatever she'd had, and there was no way she could walk out and leave him alone. Not after he'd rescued her and taken her in.

Still, she really couldn't go on accepting his hospitality much longer.

Not that she was particularly eager to leave. Having discovered a latent talent for caregiving, she was beginning to enjoy the role. An only child herself, she'd always wanted children. Hubert had said, ''Wait until I get the practice established.'' And then it was ''Wait until we pay off the house.'' After a while she'd lost her enthusiasm. Hubert would have made a terrible father. He was selfish. He had no patience. She couldn't even go to bed with a simple case of cramps without his faking some ailment that required her to get up and wait on him hand and foot. Like some long-suffering martyr in Armani suits, he'd once hobbled around on crutches for days when she happened to know there wasn't a darned thing wrong with him except for a toenail fungus.

When it came to fungus, Hubert was in a class by himself.

He *was* a class by himself.

Trav was asleep when she got back, so she swept out the sand they'd tracked in and washed their muddy clothes, selecting a few of her own to throw in with them. The bad thing about cashmere, as much as she loved the feel, was that it wasn't machine washable.

She made soup. Not the thin kind her mother liked to serve with a slice of lemon floating on the surface, that was always cold before you could get to the bottom of the bone china soup plate, but something rich and thick and nourishing. Comfort food.

At one stage of her ongoing saga, she'd gotten hooked on cookbooks. There was something comforting in reading about food.

Several pounds later she'd switched to exercise and physical fitness books, which hadn't lasted any longer than her other enthusiasms.

Humming as she worked, she added seasoning, tasted and added more—her taste buds still weren't back to normal. Now and then she peeked in at Trav, unaware of how often she did it. Or how long she lingered to watch him sleep. Once she saw that he'd flung one naked arm over his head. He wasn't wearing a shirt, or even a pajama top, so she tiptoed in and tucked his arm under the covers.

And tried hard to ignore the latent feelings that were beginning to stir just under the surface. While Trav slept on through the next few hours—while his unfinished, half-furnished house filled with the savory aroma of ham and tomatoes, onion, corn and beans—Ru reopened a few of the cartons that Trav had retrieved from the trunk of her car before it sank.

She'd packed hastily, throwing things into the banana boxes she'd begged from the food store. The framed photographs were on top of the first box. She studied them for a long time, trying to stave off the surge of feelings they aroused.

This is what it had come down to. A few books, a few pictures, a few mementoes, most of which Hubert had refused to allow her to display.

Like the vase she'd won at the state fair the year she'd graduated from high school. She'd started to toss it each time she moved, but could never quite bring herself to do it. Maybe she instinctively needed a reminder of a time when life had been happy and carefree.

A time before she had fallen for a handsome face and a glib tongue, both of which had disguised a total lack of moral fiber.

A time before her father had stunned everyone by being one of three men indicted in a stock swindle. Before his death of a heart attack before he'd even been convicted, and her mother's remarriage to a man Ru had never even met.

Before the breakup of her own marriage and all that had followed.

"Quit whining, Ruanna, you're such a limp wimp," she muttered, jamming the vase back into a corner of the box, between a stack of summer blouses and the quilt a great-aunt, now deceased, had given her for a wedding gift, which Hubert had called "hopelessly tacky."

Deliberately shutting off the flood of unhappy memories, she marched back into the kitchen and stirred her soup. Maybe the restaurant needed an apprentice chef. It couldn't be any harder on the feet and back than waitressing.

She had to do something and do it quickly. She was beginning to get a little too comfortable in the house of a stranger. If there was one thing she was determined to do, it was stand on her own two feet from now on. Not that she had much choice. She had run out of family, and except for a few from her college days, her friends no longer knew her.

No more depending on ex-husbands who refused to offer her the time of day, much less a word of professional advice.

"What's that stuff I smell?"

Trav appeared in the doorway, looking lean and mean and damp around the edges. He'd cut himself shaving. He was scowling at the pot on the stove, as if he didn't trust her not to poison him.

"Oh, for heaven's sake, I found a soup pot so I made soup. If you don't like it, feed it to Skye."

"I didn't say I didn't like it."

"What ails you—other than a nasty disposition, that is? Are you really having a relapse?"

"No, I'm not really having a relapse. I'm just not used to having strangers take over my kitchen and make themselves at home." Seeing the stricken look on her face, he could have cut off his tongue, but it was too late. "I didn't mean that the way it sounded, Ru."

What he meant was that seeing her that way, in his house, in his kitchen, looking as if she belonged there, sent his mind careening off in a dangerous direction. A number of dangerous directions. Flat-out scared the hell out of him, in fact. "Soup's nice. I like soup."

"Lovely. You can have it with my blessing as a token of my appreciation for all you've done."

Oh, hell. She wasn't going to give an inch. Not that he could blame her. He had all the finesse of a rusty sledgehammer. "I smell garlic. Didn't I read somewhere that garlic was good at keeping fleas, germs and vampires away?"

"I don't know about fleas or vampires, but garlic and onions are supposed to be good for breaking up colds."

He thought he detected a slight twitch at the corner of her mouth, but she still refused to look at him. Nose in the air. Independent as a hog on ice. "Speaking of colds, how's yours?" He tried for a casual note, but his acting skills were on par with the rest of his social graces.

"Just fine, thank you."

She held the fort for another few beats, then she gave up. He knew the minute she laid down her arms. First the gleam in her eyes, then the twitch at the corners of her mouth.

And then she was laughing, and he was grinning, sore throat and all. And neither one of them knew exactly why.

Five

Trav set the table, using stainless steel and heavy white crockery bowls that were practically indestructible. He wished he had a tablecloth to cover the ugly pink laminate, but Sharon had taken the linens, along with the silverplate and china.

Not that he'd begrudged her the wedding gifts that had come mostly from her friends.

Trav had friends, too, but they were more the type to give a case of whisky or tickets to a boxing match. A few of them had. Sharon had never let him forget it.

He was no good with women. Oh, he got on well enough with the women he'd worked with. He did his job; they did theirs. There were guidelines to follow. He'd never had any trouble following the rules when he knew what those rules were, but when it came to women outside the service, there were no rules. They seemed to operate under a code all their own. A code he had never been able to crack. Sharon had complained that being married to him was like being married to a piece of office furniture.

After thinking it over he'd decided she was probably right. Office furniture had a purpose. No one expected a file cabinet to serve as an armchair. A desk couldn't be expected to double as a bed.

From the very first day of their marriage, she had set out to reinvent him. It hadn't worked. He'd tried to please her, but he couldn't be what he wasn't. He'd thought it was enough to be dependable, hardworking, sober and faithful. He had tried his best not to allow any selfish dreams to interfere with day-to-day reality.

It hadn't been enough for Sharon. It hadn't been enough for Kelli. Thank God that with Ru there were no expectations to live up to. They were chance-met strangers, even though they happened to be sharing a house temporarily. Ru expected no more of him than common courtesy and a few basic comforts.

It was a remarkably freeing concept.

"Coffee, milk or water?" she asked.

"Coffee." He got out the stainless steel tablespoons that doubled as soupspoons.

"Anyone ever tell you you drink too much coffee?"

"It's been mentioned a time or two."

"Make that a time or three."

He could've chosen to let it irritate him, but he didn't. The lingering aftereffects of their shared laughter, probably. It occurred to him that he hadn't laughed a whole lot lately.

It also occurred to him that he might've allowed his guard to slip a few notches. He'd even permitted himself a few fantasies of a sexual nature, knowing he was safe enough because nothing was going to happen between them. They'd been thrown together, but only on a temporary basis. She had her agenda; he had his own.

And his was centered on Matthew. On getting to know him, building the kind of home he could be happy in, learning to be the kind of father to his son that his own father had never even tried to be.

Shape up or ship out, kid!

Brace those shoulders, boy, or I'll do it for you!

Avery Holiday had been good at barking out commands, and not above enforcing them with the back of his hand. As a role model, he'd been lacking in several areas. Mostly, he'd been absent.

Things were going to be different with Matt. They'd talk, get to know each other. Do things together. Teaching the boy self-respect and respect for authority, helping him through the treacherous waters of adolescence, was a tall order, especially in today's world. Trav only hoped he was up to it.

While Ru ladled the savory, chunky soup into two bowls, he flexed his shoulders to ease the tension that always seemed to gather there, and found somewhat to his surprise, that there was none to relieve.

"Do you think Skye can handle a ham bone?"

"Only if you want him to be your slave for life."

"Sounds good to me."

"We'll take it over when we give him his evening run."

We. He was going to have to tighten up on his self-discipline.

Over soup and crackers they talked about food that didn't come out of a can. They talked about pets they'd wanted and hadn't been allowed to have. They talked about music they remembered, groups they'd liked at various stages in their lives, and he was both stunned and touched when she admitted to getting teary-eyed at marching bands.

Not that he would ever admit it to a living soul, but they got to him that way, too. He'd figured it was an occupational hazard.

And then, out of the blue, she brought up the matter of her crank calls. She'd told him about them briefly, along with enough other stuff so that he hadn't been sure she wasn't stringing him along. Things like that didn't happen outside of soap operas.

"I know," she said before he could voice his skepticism. "You don't have to tell me I overreacted. Kids do that sort of thing all the time. I remember Daddy telling me about how he and his friends used to call up storekeepers and ask if they had Prince Albert in a can, and when they said yes, Daddy would tell them to let him out."

"I doubt if kids these days even know what Prince Albert was, much less who he was. Is that what you think your calls were? Kids' pranks?"

"No." She rearranged several oyster crackers on her plate, looking sad and vulnerable and trying desperately not to show it. "It was definitely a woman's voice."

"You recognized it?"

She shook her head. "I think it might have been disguised."

Which meant it could have been someone she knew. He didn't bring up that possibility. She'd probably considered it herself. "Were the calls threatening?"

She shook her head, still not meeting his eyes. "It was mostly name calling. You know—the kind of words that used to get your mouth washed out with soap. At least they did in my family."

Not in his. His mother could swear with the best of them. ''Did you go to the police?''

She nodded. ''The officer I talked to said it was probably some kid's idea of a joke. I got the feeling he had far more important crimes to solve. You'd think he could at least have let me take a number and wait.''

''Were there any more calls?''

Wordlessly she nodded.

''And did you go to the police again?''

''What do you think?'' The self-deprecating words came with the kind of smile that cut through his defenses like armor-piercing ammo.

There it was again, that feeling of protectiveness—almost of possessiveness. He raked back his chair and stood, needing to do something to keep from doing what he wanted to do. Which was to promise her everything would be all right.

Turning to the sink, he started rinsing dishes. Dammit, it wasn't up to him to promise her anything. From now on, any promises he made were going to be to his son.

But if it helped her to talk, he could listen. He'd often counseled personnel who had come to him with personal problems. ''So how'd you handle it?'' he asked, enabling but not pressuring her to continue.

''I ran away.'' She waited for him to criticize her method of coping. When he said nothing, she went on, her voice hesitant, unsure, as if she were feeling her way through a minefield. ''I didn't think of it as running at the time, but that's what it was. Looking back, I can see a clear pattern of running away whenever things started going wrong. Especially after my marriage broke up.''

He nodded, saying nothing. He knew all about bad

marriages. He didn't know what had gone wrong in hers, and didn't particularly want to know. He did know the guy had been a fool to let her go.

"Looking back," she mused, "I should've stuck it out, tried harder. I've always been too impulsive. It was one of the things Hubert despised about me. He said most of his business came from damned fools acting on impulse. Did I tell you he was a lawyer?"

Trav nodded. He was no lawyer, but he'd dealt with his share of fools acting on impulse, disregarding the rules, endangering their own lives and the lives of others, including those who ended up having to rescue them.

"I didn't turn out to be the kind of wife he expected. I don't know why—I should have been good at it. My mother was the perfect example, great at entertaining, at delegating, at all the little social remarks that pass for polite conversation. At one time or another she was on the board of just about every worthwhile charity in Atlanta."

Curiosity nudged him to ask her what kind of wife she had been. Fortunately, before he could blunder in over his head, she went on to tell him.

"We had this cook when I was growing up. I learned to bake before I was twelve. I was supposed to be polishing up my tennis game while Mama and Daddy were in Switzerland, but I broke my arm, so I pestered Mallie to teach me to cook instead. And then Achilles—he was our gardener—taught me all every debutante needs to know about compost, mulch and pruning, and about the different types of fertilizer and when to use which on what. Mama had a conniption fit when she got home, but Daddy just laughed. He said not to worry, once the novelty wore off, I'd get tired of it."

"And did you?"

"You know, I'm not really sure. I never had a chance to find out. That was the year I went off to boarding school, and after that there was junior college, and then I got involved with all the things girls do at that age. Which didn't include, unfortunately, learning anything even faintly useful. Unless you count learning how to keep a perfect crease in my blue jeans."

She looked at him and burst out laughing, and Trav felt another fault line form in his once impregnable defenses. Good thing she wasn't going to be around much longer.

"My first mistake was marrying right out of school. By the time I found out that Hubert—well, there's no point in going into all that. The thing is, I was lucky to find work at all after my marriage broke up. Thanks to Achilles, I got a job in the plant nursery where he used to buy all our supplies. Poor old Achilles, he was horrified the first time he saw me there after he'd gone to work for one of our neighbors. Anyway, I waited tables during the day and repotted plants at night. That was after I gave up on becoming a paralegal."

"A paralegal. Did I miss something?"

Ru saw the way he was looking at her. Fortunately for her tender self-esteem, he was too polite to say what he was thinking.

"Yes, well—since degrees from small junior colleges don't create a lot of interest in the job market, I thought I'd give it a shot. Going home wasn't an option. By that time, neither of my parents was in any position to help."

She started to speak, shrugged, and said simply, "No point in dragging out ancient history. What's done is done, and now there's nowhere to go but forward."

"Damn the torpedoes, full speed ahead," he said softly.

"Couldn't have put it better myself." Her smile held the self-deprecatory kind of humor that touched him like no woman's smile had in a long time.

"So why not just get an unlisted number? Why let some nut drive you out of town?"

"Actually, by that time, there was another reason to leave town. I'd moved twice, and the calls kept following me, and on top of that, I had this problem with my credit cards."

Trav knew about women and credit cards. Both Sharon and Kelli had had the same problem, as did several of the Coasties he'd worked with.

"Someone got hold of my social security number and used it to get a new driver's license, new checkbooks and credit cards, claiming theirs had been stolen. Before I even realized what was happening, I was in debt over my head and in trouble with the law for all kinds of violations, and—"

"The hell you say. You mean, all this was done in your name?"

Wordlessly she nodded. He'd thought a busted marriage, a busted car, a few crank calls and a missing friend were bad enough. What the hell had this lady done to deserve all this?

Feeling guilty for making a snap judgment on insufficient evidence, Trav massaged the back of his neck, where tension was beginning to gather again. "Now, let me get this straight," he said, and proceeded to go into everything she'd told him, point by point, starting and ending with the phone calls. He might not be the world's softest touch, but he did have an organized mind.

"And you think it's all related?" he finished up.

"The calls and the rest of it? I don't know what to think. All I know is that things started happening a few months after Daddy died, and a few months before I walked out on my husband. With all that on my mind, I finally reached the point where I didn't know where to turn or what to do. It's taken me more than two years to get my finances straightened out again. During that time, my divorce settlement was signed, sealed and delivered. Guess who won and who lost?"

The bastard. Trav wanted to hit somebody. Instead, he jammed a fistful of cutlery into the dishwasher.

"In a way, I suppose the calls were the least of it, but they certainly didn't help. I relocated twice. I did get an unlisted number, and I even went so far as to call my ex-husband's office and ask for help when the calls started up again."

He swore softly. She nodded and said, "My very words."

"Okay, next question—why'd you wait so long to take your friend up on her job offer? You said she'd made it shortly after you broke up with your husband."

"Lousy timing? Oh, I don't know—I guess at the time, it sounded more like a beach vacation than a serious career option. Moe and I roomed together in college. She's from Virginia. Her folks had a place down here somewhere, but I think it got washed away a few years ago."

Trav nodded and waited. He didn't really need to know all this, didn't know why he kept digging. He didn't need to take on someone else's troubles.

"I haven't talked to her in…goodness, it's been almost a year. I guess I should've checked first to see if the offer was still open."

Minor understatement. ''Yeah, a little advance warning might have been in order.''

Ru nodded and dumped another spoonful of sugar in her tea. She liked it two-bag strong, with milk and sugar. It was a comfort food that dated back to when Mallie used to treat her scrapes, scratches and childish disappointments with hot tea and cinnamon toast.

''Anything else? You might as well get it all out in the open. It helps to know where all the hidden shoals are when you're trying to chart a new course.''

''Did I forget to mention that I'm allergic to cashew nuts? And that I can't stand elevator music?''

''Duly noted. No cashews or elevators on the premises. I'll see that it stays that way for the duration.''

The duration of her stay. Which wouldn't be much longer. The words went unspoken, but they were there, all the same.

Ru left her unfinished tea on the kitchen table and stared out the window over the sink.

A few minutes later Trav got up, thanked her for the meal and headed for the corner bedroom to nail up a few more boards. Somewhere outside, a dog barked. The sound of an outboard motor could he heard in the distance. Ru wondered if Miss California liked ham bone soup, and decided she might as well take the rest of it over to her house along with Skye's bone. It was something to do until Trav was ready to drive her to Hatteras to see if she could find out anything about Moselle, or at least see if she could afford to rent a motel room.

As it turned out, Trav's neighbor welcomed the soup, welcomed the company even more. ''Come set and talk a spell,'' she invited, and then did most of the talking herself. About Travis Holiday.

"He's a good boy. He's not a native-born Banker, but some of his folks come from just over onto the mainland. Lawless stock. I used to know a Lawless back when I was a girl. He come out here to the Banks with my third cousin on my pappy's side. Had a great big mustache, he did, and a smile that'd sizzle your gizzard. I weren't half bad meself in them days. Dance? Lawsy, with Edgar playing his fiddle, I could dance till the rooster crowed."

By the time Ru got back, Trav had finished one complete wall, washed up and changed his shirt for another black flannel just like the one he'd changed out of except for the streak of orange paint on the sleeve.

Clothes didn't make the man, the man made the clothes. Hubert, with his carefully styled hair and his designer suits, couldn't hold a candle to a man like Travis Holiday.

In fact, there weren't any men like Travis Holiday.

Trav called Miss Cal to tell her that one or both of them would be over later to run the dog for her. Then he turned to Ru and suggested a sight-seeing trip. "The roads are in pretty good shape. You might want to look around, sort of get your bearings before you make any long-term commitments. Not everyone can handle an Outer Banks winter. It can get pretty rough."

"Believe it or not, we have snow, even in Atlanta."

"I'm not talking about the weather. In case you hadn't noticed, there's not a whole lot going on this time of year. You won't find much in the way of entertainment. Some people can't handle the isolation."

"Well, we'll see, won't we? If I start screaming and clawing at the door, you can put me on a bus to Atlanta."

"Sorry, no public transportation."

So he bundled her up and drove her to the lighthouse and parked, with the wind whistling in off the Atlantic. "Tomorrow the wind'll likely fall off. Temperature might even make it into the sixties."

She scoffed at that, and he grinned, wrinkles fanning around his eyes. "About the only constant here on the Banks is change."

For several minutes they gazed in comfortable silence at the spiral-striped tower that was a symbol of strength and endurance. A short distance away on the other side of the dunes, the ocean lapped greedily at the shore.

In the steamy interior of the truck, which smelled like oil and leather and that subtle spicy fragrance she wore, he thought about how vulnerable this narrow strand of barrier islands was, and how long it had endured. About how vulnerable even the strongest among men were. About the difference between desires and basic human needs, between simple contentment and the kind of restless discontent that could drive a man to do foolish things.

But he didn't say anything because he'd never been comfortable for very long thinking about abstract concepts, much less speaking about them. A philosopher he was not.

When he figured she'd seen enough, he switched on the engine and drove down a few of the back roads of Buxton, then headed through Frisco on down to Hatteras, where he located her friend's rented house. The sun-faded shutters were tightly closed. There was a deserted look to the place, with its wild vines and straggling runners of St. Augustine grass trying vainly to cover the sandy patch of lawn. A black plastic garbage can was lying on its side near the carport, victim of dogs, raccoons or the wind. On one side of the front stoop was a foil-wrapped flowerpot holding the remains of a dead poinsettia left over from Christmas.

Depressing. He hadn't really wanted to depress her, but she might as well see the island at its least hospitable if she planned on sticking around.

"Seen enough?" he asked quietly.

Ru nodded. She'd seen more than enough. He drove her by the restaurant where Moselle worked as an assistant manager, and she stared at it for all of thirty seconds before she'd had enough of that, too. If the sun had been shining brightly she could have dealt with it more easily. On bleak days like this, when the sun never quite managed to break through, she'd much rather curl up with a cup of tea and a good book than deal with the hard facts of life. But then, that was a luxury she could no longer afford.

"While we're out, do you suppose we could drive by a motel and let me run in and see about a room? Nothing too luxurious."

"You don't have to do that."

"I've imposed on your hospitality long enough, but thanks. It's sweet of you to say that."

"Now, there's a first," he muttered, and she thought he must mean the compliment. She found it hard to believe no woman had ever complimented him before. He wasn't smooth, not the way Hubert had been, buttering his way through life with outrageous compliments.

He was a lot more honest, though, and that was a quality she had learned to value above all else. And besides, he really was kind. She'd watched him with Miss Cal and that wild, headstrong dog of hers. Hubert wouldn't have given either of them the time of day, yet

Trav looked after the old woman with no thought at all of any possible advantage to himself.

It might not show at first glance, but he was sweet. Watching his large, callused hand on the gearshift, the subtle flex of muscles under his worn jeans as he clutched, shifted and reversed in the middle of the street, she thought he was more than sweet, he was sexy as the very devil.

And *that* was certainly nothing she intended to dwell on.

"You're sure you want to do this? You know you're welcome to camp out at my place as long as you need to."

It took all her strength of character to insist. "It's the least I can do, after taking advantage of your hospitality for nearly a week. Not that you had much choice in the matter."

"Sure I did, I could have called emergency rescue and had them come pick you up. I could have dropped you off somewhere along the way."

"Where, at the nearest homeless shelter?" In a place this small, there probably wasn't one. Turning as far as her seat belt would permit, Ru studied his long, square jaw, now slightly shadowed. His nose was large, but the crook didn't show from the side, nor did the intense blue of his eyes. Strictly speaking, he was far from handsome, yet there was something about him—something so stunningly masculine, so attractive, she knew she'd do well to get away before she lost what few wits she had left.

He pulled into a motel parking lot, empty but for two trucks and a Mercedes with a New York license. There wasn't a soul in sight. Bracing herself, she went inside and interrupted the clerk, who was watching a basketball game on TV.

A few minutes later, after a depressing exchange with the desk clerk, who was also the proprietor, she turned to go. There were plenty of rooms available, but even at the winter rates, her funds wouldn't last a week. She'd offered to work. To clean rooms, help out in the kitchen or dining room or at the desk, only to be told that there were no dining facilities, and what little needed doing, he and his wife did.

"This time of year, it's about all we can do to scrape by," the man had said. "Storm ruined the best part of last season. We had a bunch of repairs to make. Sorry, miss. Wish I could offer you something, but you see how it is."

She saw. Saw that she needed a job and she needed it quickly. Saw that she should have thought things through before she'd packed up and left town. There wasn't even a fast-food place here where she could flip burgers and buy her meals at a discount.

Trav was waiting outside the door for her. For a minute, from the way he looked at her, she thought he might have overheard, but she was too discouraged to let a little thing like embarrassment get the best of her.

What she needed now was a nap. A cup of tea, strong, hot and sweet, and then a nap. Evidently it took more than a few days to recover from this particular version of the flu.

"Tired?" he asked.

"Just drooping a bit. Give me a minute, I'll get my second wind."

By all rights he should be drooping, too. He'd had less time to recover than she had. Instead, he looked tough, enigmatic, relaxed the way a cat relaxed, ready to spring into action at the first sign of danger. He must have the constitution of an ox.

They were headed north when another pickup truck approached from the opposite direction. Trav slowed down, as did the other driver, until both trucks were stopped side by side in the middle of the highway. Both drivers rolled down their windows. Trav said, "Rance," in that way men had of acknowledging one another.

"Trav." The red-haired, red-faced man in the red-checked shirt nodded. He didn't look like a potential employer, so Ru leaned back, closed her eyes and allowed her mind to drift.

She could just hear her mother's old gang greeting each other that way at their Thurdsay golf luncheons. "Verlie. Mary Louise. Sara Ellen. Hattie." Followed, of course, by the obligatory air-kiss.

Red-shirt spoke up. "I dropped off half a peck at your place. Left 'em on the front stoop."

Half a peck? Was that Islandese for a social kiss?

She grinned, eyes still closed, as Trav said, "Much obliged."

"Joe said to tell you he can't come until next week. Martha's got an impacted wisdom tooth. He took her to Norfolk."

"No problem. Anything I can do?"

"His boat's tied off up the creek. I'm feeding his geese."

"Let me know if you need a hand."

"Will do."

Both men rolled up their respective windows. No "Goodbye," no "See you around." No introductions. Not that Ru had expected one. She was feigning sleep, after all. Lulled by the drone of the heater, she could easily have drifted off into the real thing.

It was called the line of least resistance.

It was also called escapism.

They drove the next few miles in companionable silence, wrapped in warmth from the noisy heater. The wind picked up, flattening the sea oats against the dunes. They passed two more trucks, each with a dog in the back, then a rusty Blazer with a bumper full of rod holders. Trav greeted each driver by lifting one finger from the steering wheel.

He was *not* a demonstrative man. Yet, somehow, she sensed that he was not at all an unfeeling man. Interesting combination, she mused. Still waters run deep, and all that....

Sexy, funny, caring, her mind filled in before she could switch it off.

Cut that out, Roberts. Behave yourself!

No matter how much she might be tempted to lean on any man, either physically or emotionally, it wasn't going to happen. If there was one lesson she had learned—and actually, she'd learned several over the past few years—it was the value of independence. She wasn't there yet, but she was getting closer. Except for the flu thing, she felt stronger than she'd felt in ages. If she'd had to be rescued by a man, she could have done far worse than to be rescued by a man like Travis Holiday, who was not a man to suffer clinging vines.

In some ways he was a lot like his house. Strong, unpretentious and dependable. Unlike the handsome whitewashed brick house in Druid Hills where she'd grown up. She'd always loved it because it was home, but it really was pretentious.

It was also no longer hers, having been sold to help pay her father's lawyers.

So much for home and family. Her own pedigree was

impeccable—her family had belonged to all the best clubs, married into the right families, joined the right church, supported the right charities—and none of it had mattered in the end.

According to Miss Cal, the only family Trav possessed consisted of a son he'd never met—there was a story there, but she had an idea she wasn't going to hear it—and a couple of distant cousins he'd never even heard of until recently.

Strength was what mattered. Strength of will, of character. The strength to survive hardship and help others along the way. Her father had been that kind of man, known for his philanthropy. He'd never raised his voice to her, much less his hand. She would always love him, but…

"I'm going to shuck the oysters Joe left and take a mess over to Miss Cal. You like yours raw, fried or stewed?"

"Uhhh…"

"No need to make up your mind right now. Go on inside and warm up." Reaching across the seat, he buttoned up her coat, tucked her hair behind her ears and then patted her knee.

Patted her knee! There wasn't anything even faintly sexual about it, it was pure kindness, pure impulse.

Oh, Lordy, don't let me like him too much. Don't let me do anything really stupid again.

"How does a fried oyster sandwich sound to you?"

It took her a minute to pull herself together. Parked close to the house, the truck's engine ticked as hot metal cooled in the late afternoon air. "Um…interesting?" she ventured.

He chuckled. "Is that a polite way of saying you're not too enthusiastic?"

"It's a polite way of saying I'm willing to give it a try."

It was a polite way of procrastinating. He hadn't asked her if she'd reserved a room at the motel. If he asked, what could she tell him? That she couldn't afford more than a night or two, and if Moe didn't show up pretty soon, she didn't know what she'd do?

However, he'd mentioned supper, and after that there was that lumpy, ugly couch of his, which, right now, was beginning to look amazingly inviting. "As long as you have plenty of ketchup," she ventured.

"My favorite vegetable," he assured her solemnly, and then, there it was again. That crazy urge to laugh, to share some silly bit of nonsense, some warm and friendly feeling that couldn't possibly mean anything, because neither of them was looking for anything.

Six

On the cot he had borrowed from the base and set up in the unfinished spare bedroom, Trav crossed his arms under his head and gazed up at the ceiling. An orderly man by nature, he'd been working on his postretirement plans for some time, starting with the marine communications business he hoped to develop. Since then they'd expanded to include Matt and the house. His business had been put on hold for now.

He'd wanted to go rushing off and collect his son as soon as he'd learned of his existence, but Sharon and his own common sense had stopped him. It was a delicate situation. One that needed careful handling if he wanted to get off on a solid footing.

Then, too, he'd needed a place to call home. Once the house was finished, he'd be ready. He'd even bought a hoop to mount over the shed door. If the kid ran true to form, he'd be tall. Both Trav and his father had hit six feet before their fifteenth birthday.

By then, fishing would be picking up, too. There wasn't much that could match the thrill of a run of big blues. There'd be dozens of things a boy and his father could share. He intended to give them all a try. Something was bound to click.

Which brought him to the one thing he hadn't figured on.

Ruanna. It was one thing to have a woman around when he was too sick to do much about it. It was another thing entirely now that he was on the mend and his hormones were on the rise again. Even if he'd been looking for a woman—which he wasn't after the fiasco with Kelli—the timing couldn't have been worse. Besides, it didn't even make sense, the effect she had on him. Long-stemmed, soft-spoken society types had never appealed to him. His tastes ran more to the wholesome, sexy, cheerleader type.

Ruanna had grown up in a house that sported not only a cook-housekeeper, but a damned butler. He didn't even know the breed existed outside English movies. She wore cashmere sweaters and white silk underwear without a scrap of lace on it. Which meant she wore it not for show, but because ladies were supposed to wear only the best.

Yet with all that, she was a far better sport than he'd have expected. Then, too, there were those puns. He'd never before met a woman who appreciated puns, much less bad ones.

This thing he was feeling—he'd like to chalk it up to a lowered immune system and a shared sense of humor—was more complicated than that. For one thing, he hadn't been this horny in twenty years.

There'd been a time when, like most young men, randiness had been a normal condition. As he'd grown older, he'd settled into a fairly predictable pattern. When an attractive woman signaled her willingness, he considered the situation and, if practical, acted on it. Otherwise, he took a cold shower and got back to work.

With Ruanna Roberts, she signaled nothing. If she was interested, she did a damn fine job of covering it, yet all he had to do was look at her, catch a drift of her spicy, citrusy scent, and he was instantly on full standby alert.

Battle stations.

Armed and dangerous.

Hell, all he had to do was think about her, and he was all of the above. After a virtual-reality dream involving Ru standing stark naked in a creek full of rat snakes, he'd woken up painfully, embarrassingly aroused.

Which went to show that while he might have conquered the flu bug, he was still delusional. If any woman was off limits—and until further notice, all women were—it was one who brought her own baggage. He was hauling around plenty of his own. The last thing he needed was complications of the female variety.

Waiting until he heard her leave the bathroom, Trav rolled off the low cot, stepped into his jeans and headed for a shower and shave. He'd just adjusted the water to suit him when the phone rang.

"Can you catch that?" he called through the door. "If it's Miss Cal, tell her I'll be over after breakfast."

Ten minutes later he emerged, refreshed and dressed in khakis, a clean gray sweatshirt and a pair of deck shoes that were only slightly paint spattered.

"It was your cousin Lyon. They're coming over this afternoon."

"My cousin *who?*"

"All I know is what he said. That's Lyon with a *y,* not an *i.* I asked him. How many cousins do you have named Lyon?"

"None that I know of. At least I'd heard there were a few more around, but not the names. Are you sure he said he was my cousin?"

She nodded and went on placing strips of bacon on two plates. It was done just the way he liked it—crisp without being burned.

"And he's coming here?"

"This afternoon. He was calling from Manteo, and said as long as they were this close, they might as well drive on down. He sounds nice."

Nice or not, Trav wished he could put it off. After meeting his cousin Harrison last week, it had occurred to him that a stockpile of relatives on his side of the ledger might help make up for the mother, the half-sisters and stepfather Matt would be leaving out on the West Coast. But Matt wasn't ready to meet them all yet. It was too much for Trav, let alone a kid who'd never even met his own father.

"Maybe we should warn him off, tell him about the flu."

"Too late, I've already invited them to supper. Besides, I doubt if we're still contagious. Now, sit down and eat your breakfast. They won't be here for hours."

Pressure. By now he should be used to it. There hadn't been a time in his life when he could recall being without it. If it wasn't his mother's drinking, worrying about her driving home at night, it was his father's long absences, leaving him in command.

Listen, kid, I'm leaving you in command, you hear? Look after your ma for me. I'll call when I can, okay?

Trav had taken his duties seriously. By the time he'd finished high school and enlisted, the habit had been ingrained.

"Here, have some fig preserves. Miss Cal sent them."

Absently he took the jar and spread the stuff on his toast. It could have been caulking compound, for all the attention he gave it. "You said they."

"I said what?"

"They'd be here. My cousin and who else?"

"Just his wife as far as I know. Why, does it make a difference?"

He shrugged, feeling the tightness at the base of his skull. "Dammit, I'm not set up for company."

Without responding, she stirred her coffee. And stirred, and stirred, and stirred. Trav had the grace to apologize. "Sorry, I didn't mean that the way it sounded. I don't consider you company."

He didn't know what he did consider her, and was half-afraid to find out.

"They're family. That's different," she said.

"Actually, one of the reasons I decided to stay on here after I retired is the fact that I discovered I had a few relatives in the area. I met the first one last week, but this is not a good time—"

"Too bad. You're about to meet another one, so you might as well relax and enjoy it."

"Dammit, I don't have time to relax and enjoy it! Maybe later on, once I'm settled in here—"

"Too late, they're on their way. Besides, family's not like company. They have to accept you, warts and all."

He glared at her.

"Well, maybe not warts," she amended. "At least not where they show, but they'll probably excuse your nasty disposition when I tell them you've been sick."

She smirked. It was only a smile, but he preferred to think of it as a smirk. "For your information, I'm known for being fair minded and even tempered."

"Oh? By whom?"

He snarled something that didn't make much sense and regretted it immediately. It wasn't her fault. None of this was her fault, the fact that he was running behind schedule, that he'd lost time getting his home ready by coming down with that damned bug, that his libido had chosen the wrong time to emerge from hibernation.

"Okay, so we've got company coming. Maybe if there aren't enough chairs to go around, they'll take the hint."

"You've got plenty of furniture. The sofa seats three, and we can drag in a chair from the kitchen."

A reluctant grin broke through. "Okay, so that takes care of the seating arrangement. What do we do if they turn out to be jerks?"

"We act even jerkier. That way, they won't stay long."

With a reluctant grin, he shook his head. "That ought to be easy. For me, at least. I'm not sure you could come up to scratch."

"I wouldn't bet on it if I were you. I had seven years of instruction from one of the best. Look, they're not going to be jerks, they're your cousins. They'll be perfectly lovely, just you wait and see."

"Uh-huh. 'Lovely.' It's a family trait, in case you hadn't noticed." His head was throbbing, but most of the tension had left his shoulders.

"Oh, believe me, I noticed," she said with lightly

veiled sarcasm. "Look, just relax and go with the flow. Roll with the punches. Whatever."

"Easy for you to say," he grumbled, but he was grinning broadly now. She had a way of doing that to him—putting things into perspective. "You're something, lady, you know that?"

"Would you care to be more specific?"

Slowly he shook his head. "I don't think that would be a good idea."

Busying herself at the sink, she said, "Probably just as well. I'm not sure my ego could take it."

Trav leaned his hips against one of the pink laminate counters and studied her slender backside. Funny thing how long tweed skirts, baggy sweaters and flat, lizard-skin shoes had never before struck him as sexy. On her, they were downright sinful.

Or maybe it was what those clothes covered. Warm, ivory-colored skin, understated curves and a hell of a lot more spunk than any woman in her situation ought to possess.

"Ru?"

"Mmm?"

"Stick with me for a while, will you? I could use some help."

"I'm hardly in a position to leave, unless you're ready to deliver me and my belongings to the motel." She said it with that same understated smile, but he could tell she still wasn't entirely comfortable with the situation.

Hell, neither was he, but for the time being, he needed her as much as she needed him.

And she did. Without meaning to eavesdrop, he'd heard enough of the exchange with the motel desk clerk to know that she was strapped for cash. There was no point in her paying for a room when he had room to spare.

Trouble was, she had more pride than the law allowed. He didn't want her to think he was offering her charity. But it wasn't charity when he honestly needed her help.

"We'd better plan on feeding them. I'll handle that."

"Would you mind? It doesn't have to be much, just open some cans and—"

"I'll make a list and you can do the shopping. There's time."

"You're the boss. Me, I'm just a can man."

She smiled again, and it came to him then, what he found so appealing about her. She wasn't really pretty, not the way Sharon and Kelli were pretty. Instead, she was steady and quiet. *Lovely* was the word that came to mind. It wasn't a word he used very often, at least not about a woman.

It was her sense of humor that got to him, though. It was so totally unexpected, he found himself looking for ways to lure that smile of hers out from behind the shadows in her eyes. It was like seeing the sun emerge after days of rain.

Watch it, Holiday, he told himself. You're getting into pretty deep waters.

"I'll be nailing up a few more boards," he said gruffly. "Let me know when you come up with a list."

"I'll get on it right away. And, Trav? For what it's worth, your cousin sounded really nice."

"Yeah, well…we'll just have to wait and see, won't we?"

"You can put up with anyone for a few hours. Look how long you've put up with me."

"No big hardship. You're a nice lady."

She whistled softly. "A nice lady? Didn't they teach you anything about political correctness in the service? There's no such thing these days as a lady. I think you're supposed to go directly from girl to woman about the same time you outgrow braids and braces."

He wondered what she'd been like as a child. Braces and braids and knobby knees? Had there been shadows in her eyes, even then?

Somehow, he didn't think so. "What about 'nice'?" he asked. "Is that still permitted?"

She shook her head, and he watched, fascinated at the subtle way her hair moved against her cheekbones. "Probably not. Too judgmental."

"How's that?"

"Whose definition of nice are we talking about? Mine? Yours?"

"I'm not sure," he murmured as the space between them disappeared. "Why not check it out?"

She was stiff at first, as if she wasn't used to being held. Which made him want to hold her closer instead of letting her go. When a woman needed holding, any officer and gentleman worth his salt would oblige.

And when a man needed holding…

He hadn't intended to kiss her. God knows he'd never claimed to be a genius, but this was a world-class mistake, even for a guy who was an expert when it came to messing up his own life.

She tasted of tea and toothpaste and bacon, plus some indefinable sweetness all her own. There was something so very *right* about holding her, kissing her, that it scared the hell out of him. But no way could he let her go. That was no longer an option.

She felt warm, fragile, soft, with an underlying strength that somehow didn't surprise him. Everything about this woman surprised him, and yet nothing did. It was as if deep down he'd always known her and was just now coming to recognize her.

You're in over your head, man. Back out while you still can.

No way.

Angling his face over hers, he felt his brain shut down as his senses took over. There was nothing at all hesitant, much less reluctant, about the way her arms went around him, her fingers pressing into the swell of muscles on either side of his spine. The breath snagged in his throat. It was all he could do not to sweep her up in his arms and carry her into the bedroom—or as far as the nearest flat surface—to explore this thing that had blazed up between them.

She was the one who broke off the kiss, but neither of them made any attempt to move apart. With her face buried against his throat, she murmured, "Did I happen to mention that I'm not exactly famous for my good judgment?"

"Yeah? Could've fooled me."

He could feel her laughter, and it set off a reaction in places that laughter wasn't supposed to affect.

"I should be used to it by now. Making dumb moves, that is."

With his hand moving in slow, hypnotic circles on her back, Ru completely lost her train of thought. Something about timing, involvement, and the way her luck had been running lately. The very last thing she needed at this point in her life was to mistake lust and propinquity for something it wasn't.

He whispered in her ear, "Forget the grocery list, I've got a better idea."

"Are you going to explain why there's no food for your guests?"

"Plenty of food." He nuzzled her ear. "Like I told you, I'm a can man. Company even gets to pick the cans."

"That's the most ridiculous thing I've ever heard."

"Yeah, it is, isn't it? Humor me though, will you? I've been sick."

"That's no excuse."

And still, neither of them made a move to separate. It felt too good. Holding and being held. Warmth, strength. Being…not alone.

"It's bergamot, isn't it?"

"What's bergamot?" she said, laughter rippling through her voice like wind through a field of wildflowers.

"The way you taste. The way you smell. I read it on your box of teabags. What d'you do, rub the stuff behind your ears? Bathe in it?"

"Something like that," she admitted. "Our old cook used to rub vanilla extract on her skin. I like citrusy things. A few drops of oil of bergamot in my body lotion, on my hairbrush—"

"In your tea," he finished for her, smiling and giving her that crinkly look that was utterly irresistible.

They stared at each other for the longest time, Trav's arms around her waist, Ru's arms around his. He was shockingly aroused. She was, too, but it was more than that. Physically she wanted him more than she had ever wanted any man, but the fact that it wasn't entirely physical was what made her hesitate.

"I think I'm going to have to kiss you again," he whispered, his voice a mere rasp against the stillness.

She had all the time in the world to escape if she'd

wanted to, but then, she'd already admitted to having badly flawed judgment. And he was there, and he was holding her, his face coming closer, those startlingly blue eyes of his the last thing she saw before the world went out of focus.

This is crazy. Trav had kissed his share of women when he was younger, but a man his age didn't go around kissing when there was no chance of its leading to sex. Kissing was a means to an end, not an end in itself.

With Ruanna, it had to be an end in itself. With Ruanna, sex would not be a casual thing, to enjoy and walk away from. And even knowing all that, he couldn't help kissing her again, and it was even better the second time around. He took his time, exploring the textures of her mouth, her lips, the silky weight of her hair on his hand.

If the pressure inside his briefs hadn't been enough to let him know he was treading on thin ice, the feel of her nipple pressing against his palm did the trick. All sorts of warning bells were going off inside his skull.

Her legs were as long as his own, and he rocked her gently against his erection, which only made things worse. He wanted her so much he could taste it. She appeared to want him, too…so why not?

The part of his brain that was still functioning supplied the answer. Because he had his priorities all laid out, and they didn't include a brief sexual liaison that stood a very real risk of getting out of control.

Because he had a lousy track record where women were concerned, and if he didn't back off while he still could, he might end up screwing up her life even more than it already was. She didn't deserve that.

Reluctantly he eased her away. "I'm sorry, Ru. That was way out of line."

"For heaven's sake, don't apologize, I'm embarrassed enough as it is. Why don't we just pretend it never happened?"

"Fat chance. How're we going to explain the heavy breathing and the, uh..."

She glanced down, up again too quickly, and he had the small pleasure of watching her face turn red.

There was no way he could get out of this gracefully. He didn't even bother to try. She lifted a hand to her hair, not quite meeting his eyes. He'd thought she was pale? She was like a rose garden, all pink and dewy, her eyes a little too shiny, a little too evasive.

She was beautiful. He'd never known a woman who did less to attract a man. Her hair wasn't styled, it just hung there, all thick and brown and shiny. She was warm and real, and a week ago he'd never even heard of her.

Travis Holiday was a by-the-book man. He dealt in logic, because logic was dependable. Logic was safe. Logic, like rules, was something a man could hang on to when the going got rough.

Nothing about this situation was logical. Or safe. He'd blundered into it, and now he was going to have to blunder his way out without doing any permanent damage.

"I hate exercise, but right now I wouldn't mind a five-mile hike on the beach," she said, fanning her flushed face with one hand.

"Good, you can take Skye for his run, only I warn you, he'll want to stop and smell everything along the way."

"What about supper?"

"Haven't we still got a few cans of ravioli?"

"You wouldn't dare."

"Why not? With enough hot sauce—"

"You wouldn't dare," she repeated.

"Okay, you win. Make a list and I'll shop, then you can cook while I run the dog."

"Sounds fair enough to me."

"Lady, you don't even know what fair is."

"No, but I know what it isn't," she retorted, and he shook his head. He wasn't going to touch that one with a ten-foot oar.

Lyon and Jasmine Lawless drove up in a mud-spattered four-wheel-drive vehicle about half past two. Ru had swept, mopped and dusted, and had a pot roast simmering slowly on the stove. Trav barely had time to wash up and change, so he didn't smell like wet dog after his beach run.

"Did you walk Splotch, too?" Ru asked as they stood on the deck to welcome their guests.

Trav's guests, not hers. This arrangement between them, whatever else it was, she reminded herself, was strictly temporary.

"Tell you about it later, after the company's gone."

After the company left, she was going to call around to every motel on the island and see if one of them wouldn't allow her to work for a room, or at least a lower rate. But that could wait. Right now she owed it to her reluctant host to play hostess.

"Nice place you've got here," called the gentleman helping a very pregnant wife down from the high seat of the Yukon.

"Glad you found it. Come on inside."

Introductions were made all around. Trav said simply, ''This is my friend, Ruanna Roberts. Ru, maybe Mrs. Lawless would like to freshen up?''

''It's Jasmine, and thanks, I sure would. One of the side effects of late pregnancy is having to 'freshen up' about every five minutes. I told Lyon the next car we buy has to have indoor plumbing, or Little Miss Muffet here—'' she patted her belly ''—is going to be an only child.''

After that there was the grand tour, which took all of four minutes for the women, more for the men, who discussed things like access panels and water softeners, septic tanks and heat pumps.

Lyon was a coffee drinker, but Jasmine asked for juice if they had it, otherwise milk.

And then they got down to the personal stuff. ''Have you met our mutual cousin Harrison?''

''Yeah, a couple of weeks ago. Nice fellow. Nice wife.''

''Gorgeous baby,'' chimed in Jasmine. ''They're already talking about giving her a baby brother in a year or two.''

They talked babies, which interested the women more than the men, who talked politics.

And then they moved on to other things. Marine communications, which was Trav's specialty, and security, which was Lyon's. What with all that, plus Trav's career in the Coast Guard and Lyon's in government security, the men had more than enough to talk about.

''The way I worked it out, Lyon and Harrison and Trav are third cousins once removed,'' said Jasmine. She was trying to reach her puffy ankles when, without asking, her husband leaned over and lifted her feet onto his lap and began to stroke them.

She sighed in ecstasy. ''Pardon us, folks, but isn't he

the loveliest man? Did you notice his eyes, Ru? It's evidently a Lawless trait, that unusual shade of blue. Turn around, Trav, let us see your eyes again.''

Both men looked around—goggled was more like it. Jasmine nodded and said Trav must have gotten his eyes through his mother, who'd been a Lawless before her marriage.

''You'll have to excuse her,'' Lyon said dryly. ''My wife's a journalist, and she thinks that gives her a license to pry.''

''Ha. Look who's talking,'' Jasmine jeered.

As if she hadn't spoken, Lyon went on in the calmest voice, ''She was an actress when I met her. She was relatively harmless in those days. Note the qualifier.''

So then, of course, they had to discuss Jasmine's varied career and how the two of them had met when she'd gotten lost in the swamp where Lyon was hiding out.

Which led to the next topic. ''Lyon's not really a spook any more, he's only a desk spook now, thank goodness, because I don't think I could bear it if he was running around getting himself blown up all over again. I tend to be emotional about those things.''

''I should think so,'' Ru murmured, trying to keep up with this fascinating couple. She had a feeling Jasmine Lawless wasn't quite the flake she appeared to be.

As for Lyon, she would reserve judgment.

Correction: judgment wasn't hers to reserve. There were three family members here—Jasmine by marriage—and another one, Matthew, on the way, and none of them were part of her family. Her father was dead, she hadn't heard from her mother in over a year, and if she were lucky, she'd never see her ex-husband's artificially tanned face again.

She might be a bit short on family, but she did have

friends. If she could ever catch up with them. She had her health back. She'd had time to put things into perspective so that, with any luck, she would soon have her life back on track.

No more credit cards, of course. And no on-line banking. One of her first purchases would be one of those desktop shredders for any scrap of paper that might contain any personal information.

As soon as possible she would move into a motel until Moe got back to town and look for some kind of work to tide her over. All she needed was enough to get by on. By now, she was used to living close to the bone, as Miss Cal would say.

If she happened to meet Trav—and in a place this small they were sure to meet eventually—why then, she'd smile and say, "Hi, how're you doing?" She might ask about Skye and Splotch and Miss Cal, and Trav would ask her how the restaurant business was going, and if she liked her job.

And she'd say, fine. She'd smile and say everything was just lovely, because she had too much pride to let him know she'd rather spend one night in his arms than spent the next fifty years with anyone else.

So much for getting her life back in order.

If that didn't mark her a born loser, nothing else in this cosmic comedy she called a life ever could.

"Isn't that right, Ru?"

She blinked at the man lounging in the corner of the cedar-paneled room, a shaft of late-afternoon sunlight highlighting the gray in his thick hair.

"I said Lyon and Jasmine will have to come back later on this summer and meet another cousin. My son Matthew's going to be spending the summer with me. In fact, he might be moving down here permanently. We're still working on the details."

Seven

"I think that went pretty well, don't you?" Trav was stacking coffee cups while Ru put away the remains of supper. There was very little left. Jasmine had reminded them that she was eating for two.

"I like them. You're lucky to have so many cousins. Both sides of my family run to only children. I kept begging for a brother or sister—or at least a dog. I soon learned dogs have fleas and shed all over the rugs. I got a fish, instead."

"Made your head swim, right?" His tone was teasing, but there was a hooded quality in the way he watched her move about the compact kitchen. Neither of them was ready to confront the physical attraction that had sprung up so unexpectedly between them.

"No, but he was pretty icky." She was getting good at using wordplay to avoid issues.

"Ouch. Am I supposed to come up with a clever remark about ichthyology?"

"You never heard of do-it-yourself puns? I give you the raw material—you make something of it?" She laughed then, and Trav reached across the center island and tugged gently on her hair. Teasing and playful gestures were a little out of his line. He'd never had much practice. Ru had a way of bringing out new facets of his personality.

So maybe he'd been wrong about this relationship business. He was turning out to be pretty good at cousins. Maybe in a year or two, once he had something solid established with Matt, he and Ru might...

And maybe not.

"Here, you'd better put this up somewhere before it gets mislaid." Ru handed him the business card Lyon had given her, which had a number penciled in where he could be reached at any time.

"Let me know if you get another of those crank calls," Lyon had told her. "It's my guess you've heard the last of them, though."

"Maybe. We'll know once I get settled in somewhere and sign up for a phone."

"She's given up by now." It was Jasmine who had probed and prodded until she'd wormed the whole story out. "You want my best guess? I think it's your ex-husband's secretary."

"DeeDee?" Ru's eyes had gone round as turtle eggs. "But we always got along fine, even after Hubert and I separated."

"I had a friend like that once," Jasmine had remarked. She and Ru had hit it off right away. "At least

I thought she was my friend until she married my fiancé.''

At that point Lyon had issued a protest, so Jasmine went on to explain, ''Well, he would have been my fiancé, only he never got around to asking me, and then I introduced him to my friend, and I ended up coming east and meeting Lyon—well, actually, I came east because I didn't want to be a bridesmaid, but then, there was my grandmother, too.''

''Your grandmother. Right.'' Out of politeness, Trav had tried to keep up with the conversation, but he'd never been good at figuring out the way a woman's mind worked.

''DeeDee,'' Ru had murmured. ''Do you know, in a way, it makes sense. I mean, she knew how to reach me, even after I switched to an unlisted number. Something was always coming up about the divorce settlement. And then, as a last resort, I went to Hubert for help with this stolen identity stuff, not that I ever managed to get through to him. He was always busy or in court or tied up in a conference or out to lunch. The jerk never even bothered to call back. You don't suppose he never got my messages, do you?'' She looked thoughtful, her silky brows puckering into a frown. ''Hmm…''

Amused, Trav had watched the realization take hold. Anybody who thought soft, gray-green eyes couldn't strike sparks had never met Ms. Ruanna Roberts.

''That little…*twit!* I should have realized! She was always so sweet to my face, but come to think about it, she used to forget to pass on messages even before we split up. Hubert used to come home in a temper, blaming me for messing up his plans—'' She broke off, shaking her head. "Well...damn," she whispered plaintively. "If she wanted to cause trouble, why do something that could've cost her her job? It was no secret we were having problems."

Jasmine had shrugged. "Who knows? Spite? Fox and sour grapes? Or is it dog in the manger? I always get the dog and the fox mixed up, don't you?"

Which made about as much sense, to Trav's way of thinking, as any of the other topics the pair of them had hashed over that afternoon. Things like layettes.

What the devil was a layette? And who was this guy, Lamas, or La Mays, they'd been talking about? He sounded like a ball player, or maybe a sports announcer.

But then, Trav had heard it all with one ear while he and Lyon discussed his idea of getting into the communications business on a small scale once he got this thing with Matt settled. That was the trouble with several people talking at once in a small room. Conversations got all snarled up, like too many fishing lines too close together when a school of big blues hit the beach.

Then Ru had mentioned the pot roast and sweet potatoes, and Jasmine had said, goody, because pregnancy made her insatiable.

Lyon had smirked. Trav had grinned.

Ru had nodded gravely, the double entendre passing right over her silky brown head. At least he thought it had.

They'd all done full justice to the meal. Trav could tell they had been dying to ask questions about just who Ru was and how she fit into his life. He'd introduced her as a friend and allowed them to draw their own conclusions.

"I'd better walk off a few thousand calories," Trav

said when they'd finished cleaning up. "You want to take a run on the beach with me?"

What he needed was to get away from this cozy, domestic atmosphere before it eroded his judgment too much.

"It's almost dark. The way my luck's been running lately, I'd probably trip on a shadow and break a leg."

Besides, when Trav said run, Ru knew he didn't mean stroll. She'd seen him running the dog. She'd stack his two legs up against Skye's four any day.

"I might go over and visit with Miss Cal for a little while," she said. "Mind if I take her the leftovers? There's enough beef for a sandwich tomorrow." She enjoyed listening to the woman's tales about heroism and hurricanes and riding out the great depression on collards and croakers. Tipped back in the slat-backed rocker in an overheated house that smelled of wood smoke, snuff, fish and greens, it was almost possible to slip back in time and pretend she was a part of it all. A part of a close-knit community.

Or a family?

That might be stretching it a bit, but after today she felt cautiously optimistic about the future. Trav had struck her as essentially a lonely man, in spite of having ties to the community, yet look how things were working out for him. A son of his own, and now cousins....

Trav insisted on sleeping on the cot again that night, giving Ru his bed. For the first few days she'd been too miserable to know or care where she slept. Now that she'd recovered except for a shortage of energy, it wasn't as easy to fall asleep.

She kept thinking about whose bed she was lying on.

Whose body had slept here before she'd barged into his life.

Whose arms had held her, whose lips had kissed her—whose hands had moved over her body, holding her against him, making her hunger for something that had never been all that good for her, even in the best days of her marriage.

Not that she'd known the difference at the time. Hubert had been far more experienced than she had. They'd both agreed that whatever was wrong with their sex life, the fault was hers alone. According to Hubert, some women had the knack. Some didn't. He'd brought home an adult video and tried to get her to watch it, but she'd been too embarrassed. And then, when she'd dared to peek through her fingers, she'd made the mistake of laughing.

He'd stormed out, muttering something about damned frigid socialites, which had also struck her as hysterically funny.

Theirs had not been a marriage made in heaven. Looking back, the high point had probably been the bridal shower, when she'd gotten stewed on sangria and giggled so hard she'd spilled her drinks when they'd thrown darts at nude male centerfolds from *Playgirl* magazine, and her dart had hit the bull's-eye.

Or rather, the bull's…

Well.

With a fresh, dry wind out of the northwest, Trav woke up feeling energized and optimistic. Sometime during the night it had occurred to him that Matt might be coming up on a spring break pretty soon, in which case there was no reason why Trav shouldn't fly out and bring him back for a visit. Sort of a trial run.

He didn't know why he hadn't thought of it before, except that he'd been so damned frustrated, writing and getting no answers, calling and just missing him every time. If Sharon hadn't been the one to tell him about the boy in the first place, he'd be tempted to think she was deliberately trying to keep them apart, but that didn't make sense, no matter how much he wanted to blame her.

''Need some help?'' Ru leaned against the door frame, looking sexy and sleepy and elegant in a pair of his jeans and something she called a fisherman's sweater. The fishermen he knew were more inclined to wear sweatshirts, T-shirts and ragged flannels.

''Sure,'' he said. He didn't need help, but because he sensed she needed to feel needed, he asked her to hold boards for him to nail, to hold one end of the six-foot rule while he measured, and to hand him whatever tool he happened to need. She was so gracious about it, he felt ashamed, as if he were somehow tricking her.

Some forty-five minutes later they both stepped back to admire the finished job. ''It's kind of ragged up at the top,'' Trav assayed. ''Ceiling's a little uneven, I guess.''

''I'm sure that's it. How about a bookshelf to help cover it up?''

''On the *ceiling?*''

''Lower—maybe a foot or eighteen inches. It'd distract the eye from any teensy little discrepancy.''

He scratched his jaw. He'd forgotten to shave again, after another restless night. For hours he'd lain awake making mental lists of all that needed doing before Matt came, but then he'd fallen asleep and his brain had promptly veered off in a different direction.

Given the choice between lying awake trying not to think about the woman asleep in his bed and falling asleep and dreaming about her, he'd take insomnia any old day. Awake, he still had some slight semblance of control over his thoughts. Not a whole lot, but some.

Dreams, though…that was something else.

"Matt will want a place to put his special treasures. I had a high shelf around my bedroom over the windows. As I outgrew my favorite books and dolls, they went on the shelf. Mama wanted to throw them out because they were dust collectors, but Mallie said let the child keep them, it was better than having to put up with wailing and gnashing of teeth."

"Wailing and *what?*"

"I think it's out of the Bible. Mallie always had a quote to cover just about any situation, even my favorite dust collectors."

He just looked at her and shook his head. It didn't help that she looked so damned good wearing a pair of his old jeans that were miles too big in the waist and too snug across the stern, with a sweater that drooped from her shoulders, skimmed the tips of her breasts and sagged around her hips.

Her hair was tied back with a silk scarf, and if she wore any makeup, it wasn't evident. But then he was no expert. If she thought a lack of makeup and fancy clothes made her any less tempting, she could think again.

He was tempted, all right. Didn't want to be, but there it was. What's more, he knew damned well she was tempted, too, and that knowledge alone ratcheted up the level of temptation until it was damned near irresistible.

"Why not build him a shelf for his models—cars, boats? Whatever little boys like to collect. I guarantee nobody will even see the cracks if you give them something more interesting to look at."

He cleared his throat and frowned. "Makes sense. I might check by the exchange and see if I can find an *Eagle* kit."

"He likes taxidermy?"

"Ship model. She's a bark, the Coast Guard training ship. We could even work together on it...that's if he's interested in that sort of thing." He said it disparagingly, not wanting to set his hopes too high. For all he knew, they might not have anything at all in common. Rollins was probably a country club type, into tennis and golf and that sort of thing.

Coming up through the ranks as a mustang, any sports Trav had been exposed to had been of a more rough and tumble variety. "So," he said, as if it didn't really matter much one way or another. "A shelf it is. I've got a few more boxes of books down in the shed. I can always use extra shelf space."

So they hauled in more lumber, and Ru helped measure and hold while Travis sawed and nailed. As it turned out, she was almost as good a helper as he was a carpenter. Together they got the job done, along with a few mistakes and a lot of shared laughter.

She credited the weather. "Isn't it amazing what a difference a little sunshine makes?" Her eyes sparkled. There was a sprinkling of sawdust down the front of her fancy-knit pullover.

"Don't count on it lasting. Where the weather's concerned, down here the only constant is change."

"Pessimist. I could have stayed back in Lawrenceville and just waited for the weather to break."

"Nah, you couldn't. Then who'd have thought about putting a bookshelf up where nobody can reach it? Who'd have helped me clear the snakes out of Miss Cal's attic?"

She shuddered. "Don't remind me. I still can't believe I actually touched a live snake."

"You like dead ones better? Hey, it's no cause for tears," he said, frowning when he saw her blinking hard.

"I think I must have a speck of sawdust in my left eye. Would you please see if you can get it out?"

Taking her face between his hands, Trav angled it toward the window and leaned close. "Hang on a minute," he said gruffly, and went after a speck of yellow pine with a corner of his handkerchief. "A-ha. Got it."

She blinked hard. Still holding her face, he kissed the tip of her nose because it was red and because it was there, and because it was safer than kissing her lips, which was what he wanted to do.

Talk about your uncharted waters.

They managed to get through the rest of the day and evening without stepping too close to danger. There was the dog to run and the mail to collect. Ru dialed Moselle's number again. She called at least twice a day. Nothing more was said of moving to a motel.

Standing on a six-foot ladder, she varnished the high bookshelf while Trav put down the baseboards, and then they treated themselves to a pizza to celebrate.

''There's still a lot to be done,'' Trav said, picking the olives off his slice and stacking them on hers.

She glanced around. ''Looks finished to me.''

''Yeah, well, next I'm going to put up storm blinds. I lucked through the hurricane season this year, but we're not out of the woods yet.''

''Figuratively speaking.''

The gleam in his eyes said it all. ''You casting aspersions on my landscaping?''

''Who, me? Would I do that?''

He had cleared out just enough branches to fit a house in between trees, and that was the extent of his efforts in that respect. ''The oaks were here first. They've got squatters' rights.''

''And besides, sand doesn't have to be mowed.''

''You got it.''

Grinning, he reached out impulsively, but his hand fell short of touching her. They were both learning to be careful that way. This thing between them, whatever it was, was manageable only as long as they both appreciated the dangers.

It was going on midnight when the call came in. Ru had taken the Asimov to bed. Trav had insisted she use the bed. Then, rather than take the cot into the room next to hers and listen to her tossing and turning all night, he'd settled down on the sofa with a pillow, a blanket and an FCC handbook. By the fourth ring he came awake and was reaching for the phone when she appeared in the doorway, looking rumpled and frightened.

''Who on earth would be calling at this time of night?''

''Probably a wrong number,'' he mumbled. ''Go back to bed.'' And then, into the receiver, he barked, ''Yeah.''

Ru watched, growing more apprehensive by the minute as his scowl deepened. ''Who is it?'' she whispered. ''Is it for me?''

''When?'' More scowling. ''Who've you called?'' Cursing. And then, ''Dammit, Sharon, why didn't you let me know as soon as it happened? No, don't give me that crap, I've got a right to know!''

Ru came to stand beside him. Every instinct urged her to reach out and touch him, to let him know that whatever the problem was, she stood ready to help in any way she could. What were friends for?

She might as well not have been there. ''Put Rollins on.''

There followed more terse dialogue, mostly monosyllabic on Trav's side. All Ru could determine was that someone had disappeared, and Trav was furious that he hadn't been told sooner.

She watched the color drain from Trav's face, emphasizing the lines that bracketed his grim mouth. His eyes darkened until they were the color of wet slate.

''What's wrong?'' she demanded the minute he hung up.

At first she wasn't sure he'd heard her, doubted if he even knew she was there. So she said it again. ''Trav, you might as well tell me. If nothing else, talking helps clarify your thoughts. Is it Matt? Has something happened to him?''

He saw her then. She could tell how hard it was, pulling his mind back to the present, to where he was instead of where he so desperately wanted to be. ''Will you go out there?'' she asked, thinking, I can stay here and look after things. I can take messages. I can...

''Matt's run away. He's been gone three—no, more like four days now. *Four—damned—days!*'' He smacked a fist into his palm, looking baffled, helpless, furious and afraid all at once.

Ru more or less shoved him down into the sofa, kicking aside the tumble of blanket and pillow and books. ''Start from the beginning. Go over everything. You're good at organizing. Do it.''

''I'm not good at one damned thing,'' Trav said bitterly.

''Then lean on me. Let me be your strength.''

It was an indication of his state of mind that her remark didn't strike him as absurd that she considered herself strong enough to lean on, or that he would ever consider leaning on anyone. He never had. He wouldn't know how, even if he wanted to.

''Have the police been called in?''

''Not until today. Yesterday. What the hell time is it out there, anyway? He didn't come home from school Monday. Sharon thought he'd caught a ride with a friend. He'd spent nights there before, but never without permission. Dammit, she didn't even bother to call and check on him!''

Ru laid a hand over his fist. ''What about his father? Stepfather?''

''Rollins wanted to go to the police right away. Sharon insisted on waiting. She said Matt had been upset, and she thought he was just trying to scare her. She said kids that age did screwy things, and that he'd been in some trouble at school.''

''So when did she start to worry?''

"Not until day before yesterday, when he missed a chess match."

"Chess?"

"Yeah," Trav snarled, feeling more out of the loop than ever. "The kid's some kind of a chess nut."

"I'm not even going to touch that one."

He gave her a blank look and then shook his head. "Do you suppose you could put on a pot of coffee while I make another call?"

Using the quiet grace that Trav had come to associate with her, she left him. While she was busy in the kitchen, he dug the card from his shirt pocket and punched in Lyon's private number.

It didn't take long to sketch out the details. Lyon asked all the right questions, then promised to get back to him as soon as he had something to report. By that time Ru was back with two steaming mugs of coffee, his smelling suspiciously of JD.

"Was that Lyon?"

He nodded. "I don't know why I called. He's in Virginia. Matt's in California."

"It was the logical thing to do. Don't forget, Matthew's his cousin, too. And considering Lyon's in the intelligence business, he's bound to have contacts everywhere. With computer linkups these days, he'll know everything the police know and more."

"Rollins says they checked with bus stations, airports and the like, but odds are just as good he hitched a ride. The highway's full of creeps. Do you know how many kids disappear every day?"

She shook her head. Trav didn't, either, but he knew it wasn't going to be easy to track down one angry, troubled boy who didn't want to be found.

Or maybe he did. That was part of the problem—without knowing why Matt had run, Trav was dead in the water. What if the kid *didn't* want to be found? Or what if he'd been kidnapped? Rollins was a pretty high roller, according to a few things Sharon had let drop.

"The cops have put taps on all lines into the house in case a ransom call comes in."

"Is that a likely possibility?"

"Anything's a possibility," he said bleakly, wanting to do something. Not knowing where to start, much less what to do.

"What did Lyon advise you to do meanwhile?"

He looked at her, the calm voice of reason in a silk nightgown wearing one of his black flannel shirts as a bathrobe. "Sit tight. Wait for a call. Either from Matt or from somebody else."

"Did Lyon think Matt might call you?"

He shrugged. "No way of knowing. Evidently the kid's all messed up. For that I blame Sharon."

"Not Matt's stepfather?"

"From what I can tell, Rollins is okay. It was Sharon's idea to keep the boy in the dark about—well, about me. About who his real father is. Matt was about a year old when she met and married Rollins. Rollins never got around to adopting him, and they never bothered to tell him about his paternity."

"But I thought—I mean, why would he come here to visit, maybe even to live, if he didn't know about you? I don't understand."

He rose abruptly, stalked into the kitchen and returned with the bottle of Jack Daniel's.

And then he poured a glass and set both glass and bottle on the metal, service green bookshelf while he paced. ‘‘I’ve been writing and calling for more than a year, ever since I learned of his existence. I sent pictures—local scenes, snapshots of my folks. Matt’s grandparents. Pictures of the lighthouse, one of a whale washed up on the beach a couple of years ago. Some of fish—a record bluefin taken last season. Hell, I even sent a picture of me at my retirement ceremony, sword and all. Like he’d be interested or something.’’

He laughed. It hurt like the shards of hell, but it was either laugh or cry. ‘‘He never got any of it. Sharon tossed it all into a box—letters, pictures, sports gear—and stashed it in her closet. Even if he did get some of the stuff, I doubt if he knew where it came from.’’

Ru made a murmuring sound that didn’t mean anything, but he felt a slight easing of the tension headache that had been growing for hours. She had that kind of voice.

‘‘I guess that’s why she told me to send money, not gifts. She said he already had most of the stuff I sent. I should have known something was wrong when my letters went unanswered and none of my calls—not a single damned one—ever got through.’’

‘‘I know how that feels,’’ she said drily, reminding him that he wasn’t the only one with personal problems.

Right, he thought selfishly, but hers couldn’t compare to his.

‘‘I know having your identity stolen and then being harassed while you’re trying to sort things out doesn’t add up to much compared to a missing son,’’ she said, as if reading his mind, ‘‘but I do know something about how it feels when the world starts crumbling and you don’t know what to do or where to turn.’’

‘‘Yeah, well…Matt’s world evidently crumbled when

he found my letters. God knows what he was doing rummaging around in her closet. Looking for cigarettes, maybe. Or maybe she'd hidden his birthday present away, I don't know. Anyhow, according to Rollins, Matt found the letters and pictures and confronted Sharon with the evidence, and that's when it hit the fan, big-time. He never came home from school that day, and Sharon figured it was because he was sulking.''

''What's been done up to now?''

''A BOLO—that is, a be-on-lookout-for notice. It's routine in cases like this. Rollins thinks Matt might be headed this way.''

''What about Sharon?''

He growled deep in his throat. ''She fell apart. Rollins said she'd taken something to help her sleep. It figures.''

''Then we'll just have to work from this end. The police there obviously haven't found anything yet, which could mean there's nothing to find.''

He raked his hands through his hair and closed his eyes, as if shutting off one sense might intensify the others. ''I can do without that kind of logic.''

''I only meant he's probably left town, and if that's the case, he might be headed this way.''

''Yeah, and he might be crammed in a Dumpster somewhere.''

''Stop it!'' She jumped up, eyes blazing. ''Just stop that this minute! This isn't like you, Travis.''

''How the hell do you know what's 'like me'?''

''Because I do, that's why. I know it's hard, but try not to think with your emotions. Try to pretend he's someone you've never met—''

''He is.''

She grabbed his fist and shook it, then unfolded his fingers and worked hers in between them. "Think. You've got a logical mind. Use it! If you're a twelve-year-old boy and you just found out that the man you always thought of as your father isn't—that the mother you've trusted all your life has lied to you and that you've got a real father in North Carolina who's been writing to you for more than a year—what would you do?"

He made the effort. She was right. He knew she was right, but it was damned hard to set aside feelings and deal only with hard, cold facts.

Ru handed him his glass and watched as he lifted it, changed his mind and set it down again. Good, she thought. He didn't need to risk dulling his wits. But he did need to shed some of the tension that was driving him up the wall, and she didn't know how to accomplish that.

Well, she did, but this wasn't the right time for it. There might never be a right time for it.

"Then just go to bed for a little while," she suggested. "When Lyon calls back, you need to be sharp and rested, ready for— The point is, you need sleep and this might be the only time you'll have."

"Sure, why don't I just relax—take a nice, refreshing nap?" His smile was deliberately nasty.

"Don't take that tone with me, Travis Holiday, I'm not your enemy. If you don't have any better sense than to wear yourself out before you even get started, then—"

The look he gave her stopped her dead in her tracks. "Kindly butt out of my business, will you?" he snarled.

"No, I won't. You know I'm right. If you weren't so

stressed out, you wouldn't say such a thing. You're far from perfect, but you're not mean."

"No? What does it take to impress you?" He wanted to tell her what he thought of her pop psychology. She didn't know him, and she sure as hell didn't know his son.

But she didn't give him a chance to say anything. Taking him by the arm, she steered him in the direction of the bedroom. "I don't want to hear any more arguments, all right? You're too close to the problem to see it clearly, and besides, sleep deprivation does weird things to one's brain."

"What's your excuse?"

"We're not talking about me and my problems now. Admit it. You're worried sick at a time when you need all your faculties in top working order. Sleep can't hurt. And it just might help. And besides, what else can you do until you find out what needs doing? Twiddle your thumbs to the bone? Sit and stare holes in the telephone? Wear the soles off your shoes pacing?"

She was right, as much as he hated to admit it. "What makes you think I can sleep?"

"Because when the body's had all it can take, it shuts down. I read that somewhere. It makes sense to me."

"That's the only thing that makes sense, then."

"Well, why not just shut up and follow orders? After twenty years in the service, you should be good at that."

That prompted a fleeting smile. A bleak one, but a smile all the same. "I'm better at giving them, but you're right. Standing by the phone won't make it ring any sooner."

She made him take a warm shower and change into

something more comfortable than denim and twill. He didn't argue, which was a pretty good indication, she thought, of how much he needed her to hold him together.

If she let herself think about how much she wanted to do just that—to hold him—she might lose her courage. Instead, she busied herself smoothing the sheets and plumping the pillows. When he cmerged from the bathroom wearing sweatpants, his hair damp, his feet bare, she gestured to the bed.

"Climb aboard, skipper. I'll man the phones while you, um—submerge. Whatever. I can't think of a simile for sleep."

A grin creased his lean cheeks and disappeared too quickly. "I love it when you talk nautical."

Ru thought, Oh, my mercy. If she'd suspected it before, she was certain of it now. She was in trouble. In way over her head—and there was nothing nautical about it.

Eight

Man, you don't need this kind of trouble, Trav told himself as he slipped under the covers. He reached for her hand and pulled her closer, so that she was off balance. Go ahead, why not finish screwing up your life. While you're at it, mess up hers, too.

It was as if the insulation had worn off, leaving all of his nerves raw and exposed. The need, the awareness, had been growing between them for days. Regardless of what triggered it—simple chemical reaction or some crazy aftereffect of the flu—he had a feeling it was about to reach critical mass.

''Close your eyes and try to relax,'' she said quietly, but she didn't try to pull away. Instead, she sat on the edge of the bed beside him.

''Easy for you to say. How d'you know they're not closed?'' The room was pitch-dark, the only visible light the brief, intermittent beam from the lighthouse sweeping across the tops of the stunted maritime forest.

"Because you're still tense."

That was one way to describe it.

He tried closing his eyes. It didn't help. He could think about sex, or he could think about Matt. Neither was conducive to sleep.

"Visualize black velvet."

Like her voice, he thought. Dark, soft, but not without a certain tensile strength. "I will if you'll lie down beside me." He lifted the covers and waited.

After a brief hesitation, she slid in beside him. "Close your eyes. Do it," she said. "Plain black velvet."

Dutifully he pictured black velvet. There was nothing plain about it. In his version, there was a woman's nude body sprawled across the velvet. A woman with brown hair, small breasts and legs a mile long.

"Can you see it?"

He grunted.

"Is it helping?"

He shifted uncomfortably. "What do you think?"

"Good. Now, let yourself drift off. It's dark as midnight and you're floating in a warm, unlit pool."

He tried. He honestly tried, but it wasn't working. Logically speaking, what was happening to him shouldn't be, not to a man of his age and experience. They were both past the stage of spontaneous combustion, but there was no other way to describe the effect she had on him. Some lessons obviously took longer to learn than others, but even the dumbest jerk ought to know better than to stick his hand into the flames after the first few times.

Back when he'd been Matt's age, he'd been too

young to know what was going on . His father was off at sea, his mother was going out every night—with the girls, she'd always say—telling him to nuke his supper, do his homework, watch an hour of TV and go to bed.

Hours later he would still be awake when she'd stumble home, reeking of alcohol and cigarette smoke. Only when he knew she was home safe did he dare let himself fall asleep.

He wondered how mature Matt was. Sharon had her faults—they both did—but at least she didn't drink. He couldn't picture Matt coming home from school and finding her passed out on the sofa, the door unlocked, the kettle burned dry, the house in a mess, and having to make supper for himself like Trav's own experience as a boy.

No, Sharon's faults hadn't been the same as his mother's. She'd been unfaithful to him, though. He didn't know when it had started, how often it had occurred, or with whom, but after coming home to find the toilet seat left up a few too many times, he'd had enough. There'd been other things, too, but by then he'd been so disillusioned he hadn't bothered to confront her with it, knowing damned well she would lie. He'd offered to go with her for counseling. He'd even gone the reconciliation route, courting her the way she liked to be courted, with flowers and expensive gifts.

It hadn't worked. They'd kept up a polite pretense for another few months, because appearances were important to Sharon. Far more important than the real thing.

As for him, he'd had too much pride to bleed in public, but with nothing left to hold them together, the end had been inevitable. He still didn't know if she'd realized when they'd split that during one of their brief reconciliations they'd made a baby. She'd said not. He would like to give her the benefit of the doubt, but he could never forgive her for deliberately robbing him of the first twelve years of his son's life.

There'd been a few other women in his life after Sharon had left. Mostly he'd filled the void with work, but he was no monk. Then, last summer, with Kelli, the opportunity had presented itself, and he'd tried for the gold ring one more time. More for Matt's sake than his own. Wanting for his son what he'd so desperately wanted for himself as a boy. The security of a close-knit family.

It wasn't Kelli's fault that things hadn't worked out. She'd blamed him, and he accepted the responsibility. Evidently, he lacked the gene for forming successful relationships.

"Are you asleep yet?"

The low, husky voice came out of the darkness, breaking into his troubled thoughts. "Trying hard," he returned softly, and he was. Trying hard to throw up a wall between them by reminding himself of all the reasons he'd be better off grabbing his jeans and hightailing it out of here.

"Me, too."

He felt her fingertips brush against his arm, slide down and engage his hand in a reassuring grip. Like a lifeline.

They lay like that for several minutes, separate but together. He could feel her body heat reaching out to him, carrying a drift of her own subtle scent. If she'd deliberately set out to seduce him, she was succeeding. He didn't like subterfuge. He'd never been good at games. He would have sworn she was above playing them, but she had to have known when she accepted his invitation and climbed in bed with him how it was going to end.

"What are you after, Ru? Do you know what you're asking for?" He didn't mean to sound angry, bitter. Or maybe he did.

"I'm not asking for anything. Sometimes I make mistakes, though. I guess this was one more in a long list of—"

"Shh." She tried to get up, but he held her back. "If it was a mistake, it was a nice one."

"Yes, well...whatever it was, you don't have to be a party to my stupidity," she said. "Let's just pretend we said good-night in the living room, and I'll sneak out of here and see you in the morning."

"You're embarrassed."

"No, I'm not. If you want to know the truth, I'm mad as a bucket of hornets."

"With me?"

"With myself...for thinking I could help take your mind off your troubles without making things worse."

After a moment he said, "I don't think things can get a whole lot worse, do you?"

None of this business was her fault. Maybe it wasn't his, either. He'd never been one for keeping score, harboring grievances. Life was what it was. You did your best to cause as little damage as possible on the way through, and if in the process, you could snatch a little happiness, you'd be a fool not to take it. "Ru, I can't make any promises."

"Did I ask for any promises?"

"No, but you should, only not from me."

"The day I ask you for anything will be the day birds swim." There was a glittery quality in her voice, as if she didn't know whether to laugh or cry.

He caught her fist and carried it to his lips. Her tears hurt him like salt rubbed in a raw wound, so he courted her laughter instead. ''Ever hear of sea robins?''

''Stop it. Just stop it,'' she whispered fiercely.

Rolling her over to face him, he tugged her into his arms and held her there because he couldn't help himself. By that time they were both breathing hard, but it wasn't from laughter, nor was it from exertion. ''Ru—if you really want to leave, I won't stop you.''

He didn't know if it was deliberate or not, but her hand was on his bare chest, her fingers twisted in the hair surrounding his left nipple. If she had any idea how it affected him, she'd be halfway out the door by now.

''Do you know, there were times during the past few years when I would have given anything in the world for someone to hold me this way,'' she confided. ''That was all I wanted, just to be held, just to be reminded that I wasn't all alone on the planet.''

''You're not alone,'' he said gruffly as his hand moved down her back, drawing her hips closer. Holding was no longer enough, if it ever had been.

''I'm truly sorry if I embarrassed you, Trav. My timing's always been wretched. Showing up at Moe's place long after she'd forgotten she invited me. Expecting a job to be waiting for me whenever I happened to show up, and now this. You'd think after a while, I would have learned to look before I leaped, wouldn't you?''

He couldn't think of a single thing to say. Testosterone wasn't known for encouraging rational thought. But when she tried to slip out of bed, he caught her by the tail of her nightgown. ''Ru, don't go. If holding helps, I'll settle for holding. God knows, I'm not in a position to turn down any offers at this point.''

The beam from the lighthouse swept across the bedroom wall, a reminder of time passing. She hesitated, then sat back down on the edge of the bed. Trav rolled over onto his side, wanting to haul her back into his arms where she belonged, but afraid of spooking her again. He told himself he was being noble. Under the circumstances, they were both pretty skittish.

He told himself that while sex was a great escape, he couldn't use Ru that way. It wouldn't be fair, not unless she knew the score. Not even then.

With that noble thought firmly in mind, he opened his mouth and blurted out the truth. "Oh, God, Ru, I'm scared sick."

She uttered a whimpering little noise and slipped back under the covers. Finding his hand, she squeezed as hard as she could, and Trav told himself he hadn't done it deliberately to get her back in bed. Never in his life had he played on any woman's sympathy.

"I feel so damned helpless. Matt could be—" He broke off, dragged in a lungful of air and tried again. "You know what it's like out there, the news is full of ugly things. The stats might be improving, but kids still disappear every day. They wind up dead, or so deep in trouble they're as good as lost. They're so damned vulnerable! How can a guy protect his child when he doesn't even know what he looks like? I could pass him on the street at high noon and not even recognize him. Do you have any idea at all how that makes me feel?"

He broke off again, swearing. The mattress shifted, and he felt the heat of her body coming at him in waves. She said, "I don't, not really. I know what it feels like to be helpless, to try to fight an invisible enemy, but a child—your own son—I can only imagine. Didn't she even send you a picture?"

"Who, Sharon? Yeah—a snapshot of a kid in a party

hat with his face all screwed up, blowing out the candles on a birthday cake. Eight candles. It wasn't even a recent picture, dammit.''

The light swept over them again as her cool fingers found his face. He held them there, against his lips, and took several deep, steadying breaths. ''She said as soon as his school pictures came back, she'd send me one, that he'd changed so much just this past year, his earlier pictures wouldn't mean anything. She got that right,'' he added bitterly.

''Children do change. Matt's what—twelve, going on thirteen? I remember that age, just barely. You're no longer a child, and not yet an adult. I don't know how it is with boys, but girls go through a lot of stuff at that age, some of it pretty scary.''

''Boys, too. Some earlier than others. Hair sprouts in strange places. Zits pop out like toadstools after a rain. Your voice goes haywire, and you can't control it. Just when you're trying your damnedest to be cool, you do something terminally stupid.''

''It happens to girls, too. Not the voice, but the rest of it.'' She was half reclining, propped on one elbow. He caught a hint of the subtle fragrance that seemed to cling to her hair, her skin, her clothes.

''Does it?''

''You bet. Like wearing three T-shirts because you're too embarrassed to wear a bra? And then imagining all the boys making fun of you because you jiggle when you play volleyball?''

''Girls don't have wet dreams.''

''Maybe not, but that doesn't mean they don't dream.''

''About sex?''

They lay there together, talking about things he

hadn't thought about in years, much less talked about. And never before with a woman, as if they were best friends.

She had to feel it, too. This odd intimacy, needy and yet relaxed at the same time. "How did we get off on this subject? But yes, if you must know, girls dream about sex, too, only some girls don't know all that much about it. I mean, the mechanics, sure—we're taught that in sex-ed, but mostly the dreams are just strange longings, intense feelings—you know."

"Yeah, I know. About strange longings and intense feelings, at least. That part doesn't change much, does it?"

Instead of answering, she said, "I can't believe we're having this discussion."

"You're the one who started it."

"I did not!"

"I was in bed, sleeping peacefully, when—"

"You were lying there scared sick, feeling helpless, ready to fly apart in all directions. I took pity on you and—"

"Ru? I'm still scared and worried, I'm just trying my damnedest not to think about it."

She murmured a soft little "Oh," and even in the darkness he knew what she would look like. She'd close her eyes in that way she had when she'd run out of steam. She'd shake her head slightly so that her hair slithered across her shoulders, and her lips would purse up as if she was trying hard to keep from speaking her mind.

And then he made the mistake of picturing her again on a bed of black velvet....

One slight tug was all it took to tumble her on top of him. Neither of them pretended it was an accident.

He wanted her there—she wanted to be there. Later on they could rationalize, but for right now, holding was in order. A little holding, a little mind-numbing sex. Anything to get him through the next few hours of waiting to learn something—

Or worse, to learn nothing.

He didn't know which one of them instigated the kiss, but it kicked off a chain reaction that swept him into another dimension, a dimension where the mind shut down and sheer animal instinct took over.

She was a tiger. He would have figured her for another kind of cat entirely if he'd thought about it. Maybe a Siamese. Sleek, elegant, a little too cool for genuine passion.

She was a tiger. Sprawled beside him when the kiss began, on top of him when it escalated out of control, underneath him, her long legs wrapped like a pair of boa constrictors around him when they finally broke off to gasp for breath.

By that time he was pushing against her. Sooner than he'd expected, rougher than he'd intended, he was inside her, and she met him halfway, hot, damp and eager, wanting it as much as he did.

Arms braced stiffly, he shuddered with the force of trying to spare her his weight, of trying to hold back the surging tide.

Not yet, not yet—hold on, make it last....

He held on. Just barely. Burying his face in her throat, he inhaled sweet, spicy woman—warm, aroused woman. He could feel her hot, slick passage tightening around his shaft. "Wait," he rasped harshly.

"I can't," she wailed. "I don't know what's wrong with me."

"You move—if you so much as twitch a muscle, it's all over."

She twitched. He groaned. And then he commenced to pound into her, all pretense of control shot to hell. She was shouting in his ear, and he heard a voice he vaguely recognized as his own, shouting back.

He never shouted. No matter how good it was, he was always careful to hang on to that last vestige of control. Now he heard the echo of his own strangled cry, and marveled briefly, but didn't try to make sense of it.

Mind-numbing sex. It was what he'd needed, what she'd offered. The trouble was, it didn't solve anything, because once the shock waves faded away, his mind refused to stay numb.

"You okay?" he croaked.

Damn. It was happening all over again. Adolescence. He couldn't control his own voice, much less his performance.

"Mmm," she murmured sleepily. Somehow, they managed to untangle assorted limbs. He could feel her raking her hair back, hear the uneven sound of her breathing. "Mercy," she whispered.

"You asking, or offering?"

"I don't know. Both, I guess." Her laughter was a soft, breathless sound that registered on every raw nerve in his body.

"I seem to remember you saying I needed sleep."

"If you can't sleep after that, there's no hope for you."

"Is that what it was supposed to be? A tranquilizer?"

"It worked, didn't it? You're already half-asleep."

He was. Willing or not, he was fading fast. "If I

happen to doze off, wake me when Lyon calls, will you?''

For an answer she kissed him on the left eyebrow. He was snoring softly before her lips lifted away.

It was barely daylight when the call came. Trav woke up alone and slightly disoriented, to the smell of coffee and bacon and sex. Not a bad way to start the day, all things considered.

The murmured sound of a one-sided conversation in the next room brought it all back in one solid, gut-crushing blow, and he reached for the phone on the makeshift bedside table. ''Lyon?''

''Yeah, I'm here. Listen, Trav—''

They talked for perhaps ten minutes. Ru got off the line shortly after he picked up, but she was at the door, looking curious and concerned, her eyes shadowed and faintly red rimmed.

''Is Lyon on his way here?'' she asked softly.

''Not yet. He can do more where he is.''

''Does he know anything?''

''Not enough.'' Trav swung his legs off the bed, naked and totally unselfconscious. ''I'll be unpacking and setting up my computer if you need anything, but first I'd better shower. What're the chances of a shot of caffeine?''

''It's made. Breakfast, too, you'll need it, whatever happens. Trav, what computer? What has Lyon found out? I want to know everything he told you.''

Closing his eyes, he fought the urge to snap back, to tell her he didn't want to waste time talking, but discipline took over. Discipline and a deep-seated reluctance to hurt her.

''There's some indication Matt's headed this way.

They think they might've traced him as far east as Knoxville. The trail ends there, but Lyon's hooked up with all the links in the chain. Something's bound to turn up before long.''

She stood there, waiting for him to go on, but he broke off, swore softly, and brushed past her, slamming the bathroom door behind him.

Ru listened to the sound of the shower and tried not to be hurt. He was sick with worry. What parent wouldn't be? The worst of it was not knowing, imagining the worst, being utterly helpless to do anything. It wouldn't help to go charging off to Tennessee when he didn't even know where to start looking. Tennessee was a big state when you were searching for one small, lost boy.

Standing at a counter a few minutes later, Trav wolfed down his breakfast. He unpacked the computer he'd been storing until he could buy more furniture, spent less than an hour setting it up on a makeshift desk, and then passed the rest of the morning waiting, sick with anxiety, for Lyon to contact him. With only a single phone line, he was afraid to stay on-line, afraid of missing an incoming call.

Ru wished she hadn't allowed her computer skills, which were minimal at best, to fall so far behind. She didn't even know how to do Windows.

She did do sandwiches and coffee, though. Every few hours she would slide a plate and a mug, or a glass of milk, on the table beside him. ''Eat or you'll go blind,'' she warned once, getting a distracted glance in response.

''Eat or your hair will fall out,'' she said when she came back for the plate, only to find it untouched.

He leaned back, kneaded the back of his neck and

gave her a tired smile. "Back off or I'll sic Splotch and his friends on you."

"Speaking of Splotch, if you don't need me for a while, I think I'll go over to Miss Cal's and see if the dog needs walking."

He didn't need her at all, they both knew that, but at least he was too polite to say so.

So she walked the dog. Or rather, she hung on to the end of the lead while Skye raced up and down the ridge, sniffing at everything along the way, turning his oddly colorless eyes on her now and then to be sure she was behaving.

She knew better than to take him out on the highway, Trav having told her about his inclination to herd any passing cars into a tidy little bunch. She tried giving him hand signals, but obviously she lacked the right accent. He ignored her and took off again, pulling her along behind him.

She got back, breathless but invigorated, to find Trav right where she'd left him, hunched over the keyboard, scowling at the screen. After convincing him to go outside and walk around the house a couple of times to get the blood flowing to his brain again, she called and told the volunteer coordinator that Trav was back on his feet after the flu, but now he was tied up in a family emergency and wouldn't be able to deliver meals.

"I'm real sorry to hear that. Anything we can do to help?"

There was genuine concern in the voice. For some reason, that brought tears close to the surface. "No, but thanks. I'll tell him you offered."

"You're that woman riding around in his truck, aren't you? Joe said he saw you the other day down to Hatteras. He said you were waiting for Moe Sawyer to get back. I heard she's due home early next week. They always do the floors at the restaurant two weeks before they open up. My boy busses tables there nights and weekends. He says they all pitch in to get ready to open. I'll let her know where you are if I see her, okay? Tell Trav I said hey, and let me know if y'all need anything.''

Ru did her best to sort it all out. Moselle was on her way home—or soon would be. Somehow, that seemed almost anticlimactic. As for the restaurant floor, she hadn't the slightest idea what that was all about, but if part of the duty of an assistant manager was scrubbing, or waxing, or steaming carpets or whatever it was they did to the floors, heaven only knows what her own job might be.

When Trav came back inside again, his face flushed from the sharp northwest wind, she was ready to pounce. ''Here, drink this, it's good for you. Now, tell me everything that happened while I was out being made a fool of by that silly dog.'' She handed him a milkshake made with bananas, chocolate milk and peanut butter. He needed the energy.

He managed a grin that might have convinced a stranger. It didn't convince her. He was hurting badly. ''Everything?''

''Everything. Start at the beginning.''

''At least we know where the beginning is. What we don't know is where the end is. A kid answering Matt's description bought a bus ticket to Knoxville.''

''And—''

''And he could have gotten off anywhere along the line. The bus he was on ran into an eleven-car pileup just east of Nashville on I-40. The passengers were transferred to another bus, but I don't think anyone was checking tickets.''

''Do you have family in Tennessee? Does Sharon?''

''As far as anyone knows, Matt doesn't even know anyone from Tennessee. Near as we can figure, he's headed this way. Sharon said he was really pissed when he found those letters. Wouldn't talk to her. Locked himself in his room. She figured he'd sulk a day or so and then snap out of it.''

''Obviously she figured wrong. I'm sure Lyon's circulated his picture by now. Does anyone at the bus station in Anaheim remember him?''

Trav shook his head. ''A lot of kids ride the bus. It's cheaper than flying. And yeah, there's a picture out there, but Sharon says he's shot up several inches since it was taken. She says he's lost a lot of baby fat in the past few months, even in his face—so he looks different.

''What color is his hair?''

''It looked dark, like mine.''

''Yours is gray.''

That got a genuine grin out of him. ''Yeah, well...''

''What about his eyes? Blue like yours? Pink? Brown?''

''Actually, she didn't say. They don't really show up much in the picture, but I'm pretty sure they're blue. Holidays run to dark blue eyes. My dad's were light, but my mom's were the same color as mine.''

''He might take after Sharon.''

''Sharon's are blue, too. Lighter, though. She's blond. Her folks are Swedish, second generation. As near as I can tell from the snapshot, Matt's sort of a mixture. He's wearing a Raiders sweatshirt, and he's got a nice tan. Good-looking kid from what I can tell.''

"I wonder who he got that from?"

Sobering suddenly, he smacked a fist into the palm of his hand. "God, I can't take much more of this waiting!"

"Yes, you can," she said quietly. "You can take whatever you have to take. You're a mustang, and that couldn't have been easy."

She'd scanned some of his books, enough to know that he'd enlisted, gone through boot camp and eventually, been commissioned as a warrant officer. After his promotion, he'd competed on equal footing with men who'd attended the Academy or Officer Candidate School.

"The important thing is that you're right here, so that he can find you. You've got to be patient, because it takes a while to get here. Frankly, I thought it was going to take forever, and I only came from Georgia. Just think how Matt must feel, coming all the way from California."

They both fell silent for a few minutes, each lost in thought. Oddly enough, there was no constraint between them after last night. Ru would have expected a certain amount of self-consciousness at the very least, but Matt's situation overshadowed all else.

She shoved a glass at him and said, "Drink your milkshake and then go run a few laps up and down the highway. The fresh air will clear your head."

"I've already had a dose of fresh air. There's nothing wrong with my head."

"I'm not going to touch that one, but we both know you need to unwind before you explode."

"I can think of other ways to unwind," he said, a sly grin easing the lines around his eyes, deepening the ones beside his mouth.

''It's barely three o'clock in the afternoon.''

''So?''

''So—'' She broke off, blushing, of all things. She hadn't blushed since her sophomore year at college. ''Oh, for heaven's sake, go run yourself a marathon, you need it. I'll be here to answer the phone.''

Nine

Funny thing, the way a guy could pick up a habit without even realizing it, Trav thought, his sneaker-shod feet pounding softly on the narrow bikeway alongside the highway, oblivious to the halfhearted drizzle. Somewhere along the line, Ru Roberts had turned into a habit. Like the habit of sugar in his coffee and Texas Pete on his eggs. Like the habit of flexing his shoulders when he got out of bed every morning.

Like the habit of breathing.

In a remarkably short time he had grown used to having her around, hearing her move about in his house. Watching the way she frowned when she was reading or bit her lip when she was trying not to laugh. The way she hummed under her breath when she was working, and the way she lifted her face, closed her eyes and breathed deeply every now and then when they were outside. Tasting the air, she said. She was surprisingly sensuous that way.

She made little puffing noises with her lips when she slept. He hadn't slept with her all that many times, but he'd watched her sleep, watched her mutter and puff while she dreamed. Evidently, her dreams were a hell of a lot more peaceful than his.

Yeah, she was a habit. One he'd never intended to pick up, but one that was going to be hard as hell to shake.

Trav had pretty much given up on women. Love 'em and lose 'em, that was his style. When it came to establishing any kind of permanent relationship, he was a total washout. Always had been. Maybe it depended on what a man was looking for in a woman.

Or what a woman was looking for in a man.

Not that either of them was even looking, in this case.

He'd be the first to admit that his priorities had been pretty juvenile when he'd first met Sharon at a party in New London, Connecticut, shortly after he'd made chief. Full of piss and vinegar, proud of his new rank, he'd been randy as a rooster. He'd backed into her accidentally, spilling her drink down the front of her dress, and when he'd clumsily tried to mop up the damage, she'd told him he could drive her home to change, instead.

He had. They'd never made it back to the party. By the time he'd left her apartment the next afternoon he'd been head over heels in love. Half the men on the base had been in love with her. He still didn't know why she'd chosen him, but she had. Two days later he'd proposed.

After an intensive, expensive three-week courtship, she'd said, "Sure, why not?"

He hadn't been smart enough to realize that when a woman said, "Sure, why not," she meant only until something better came along.

With Kelli, his motives had been more pragmatic. The way he saw it, having a wife would make things easier when it came to staking his claim to his son. He'd leveled with her, right from the first. She'd told him he was real sweet.

Sweet. Yeah. Two months later, in the middle of overseeing the plumbing and heating in the house, he'd declined her invitation to join her on a skiing trip—one he was undoubtedly paying for. She'd thrown a doozy of a tantrum, telling him she needed more out of their relationship than he was offering.

Or as she'd put it, "Get real, Trav—you don't want a wife, you want a baby-sitter."

By the time Ru came along, he'd unofficially sworn off women, concentrating instead on making a home for Matt, getting him here, keeping him here. Rescuing a hacking, sneezing, strung-out, miserable female and bringing her home with him hadn't been a part of the plan.

Before he'd realized what was happening, he'd been up to his ears in one more doomed relationship. Stuck with another bad habit. Stuck with a woman who had a way of listening quietly when he needed to talk, fading into the background when he needed to think, forcing him with her silent presence to reexamine his thoughts from a fresh perspective.

For a woman who had pulled a dumb stunt when her own world had fallen apart, she was surprisingly sensible. Little things, such as forcing him to eat at regular intervals, to get up from his computer every few hours and work the kinks out of his body.

As if all that weren't enough, she offered mind-numbing sex when his brain threatened to short out on him, and a warm, comforting presence in his bed when he woke up in the middle of a nightmare.

Yeah, he was hooked. Didn't think much of his chances, considering his past record, but he was hooked, gaffed and all but landed.

Lyon checked in every two hours, even though there was nothing new to report. A few tips that hadn't panned out, a sighting that turned out to be a dead end. It was Ru who made him go to bed, claiming if Matt had a grain of sense—and being Trav's son, he was bound to be smart—he'd be holed up somewhere nice and warm, waiting out the weather, which had continued to deteriorate, the temperature hovering in the low thirties, wind NNE gusting to forty m.p.h., rain or snow covering the entire mid-Atlantic seaboard.

Just before daylight, the rain turned to sleet, the sound gradually creeping into his awareness. Trav always slept with a window cracked open, even in the dead of winter. He liked hearing rain beat down outside, isolating him in a private universe. Even better was the sound of sleet peppering the sides of the house and the leathery leaves of the live oaks.

He lay there and listened, deliberately holding the world at bay as long as he could. Ru was still asleep, her head on his shoulder. His arm was numb, but when she'd tried to roll away earlier, he'd held her there. He'd checked in with Lyon one last time after the late news. Exhausted by tension, stressed out with waiting, with worrying, with feeling so damned helpless, he'd only been half listening when Ru had mentioned taking a shower. He considered pouring himself a stiff drink.

If he'd thought it would help, he'd have gotten blind, knee-walking drunk, but the problem would still be there waiting for him when he emerged at the other end. A brain-busting hangover wasn't going to help much, either.

A medic had once told him he was genetically predisposed to alcoholism. He'd recommended abstinence, or if not that, moderation. Trav had opted for the latter, but he was smart enough to know that when he craved it the most, he'd be better off leaving it strictly alone.

So, desperately needing a drink, he'd done something even more self-destructive. He'd joined Ru in the shower. A clear case of out of the frying pan, into the fire. What had started there, had ended up in the bedroom. Hot, wet, soapy sex. Mind-boggling sex that had offered only a fleeting escape, but it was so sweet, so powerful, so compelling, it had quickly become an end in itself rather than a means to an end.

The first time had been over almost before it started. Burning a short fuse, he'd have taken her in the shower if he hadn't been afraid of breaking both their necks. She'd used some kind of scented bath oil, which made moving around pretty tricky, so he'd braced his feet against the sides of the tub and wrapped her long legs around his hips. Carefully, with her heat branding him on the belly, he'd stepped out of the tub, hoping he could make it as far as the bedroom before his knees buckled or he lost his priming, or both.

At least his priming hadn't suffered. Thinking back, he wasn't even sure he'd taken time to kiss her. It had been a case of instant ignition, lift off and then he'd been soaring into space. Too far gone even to look back and see if she was with him.

Eventually he'd settled back to earth. Neither of them

had spoken. He'd been too winded, not to mention embarrassed. When it came to sex, he'd always been pretty much a meat-and-potatoes guy. Get it on, get it off, end of story.

Until Ru.

He couldn't understand it—the way she affected him. The things he wanted to do to her, with her—the things he wanted her to do to him. With him. It was almost as if he were just now learning what it was all about.

She was asleep when, driven by a guilty conscience and a feeling that he'd left her unsatisfied, he'd finally gotten around to kissing her. He didn't think he'd intended to wake her, but maybe he had. At any rate, they'd ended up nuzzling and tasting, murmuring words that were mostly meaningless sounds. This was the part of sex he'd never been any good at, yet with Ru, he felt a powerful urge to try. It was almost as if he needed to tell her something without actually putting it into words.

The second time they'd made love, it was her turn. He had deliberately held back, allowing the pleasure to build slowly, like the sound of a marching band heard from a distance, the glow of a bonfire against a night sky. He'd let the heat and the throbbing beat seep into his system and held his breath while the glow grew bigger, hotter, until it threatened to blaze out of control.

Control. He had fought for it, hung on just barely, taking the time to exalt every delicious inch of her body until she was writhing, moaning, begging. By the time he'd lifted her on top of him, every muscle in his body had been clenched with the effort of holding back to allow her to set the pace.

It had damn near killed him. She'd started out tentatively, little rocking motions, circling her bottom, then rocking back and forth some more. He'd been ready to roll her and take control when she caught her breath in an audible gasp. Head back, every tendon in her throat visible, she'd gone wild.

As the action became more and more frenzied, he'd had a fleeting, subliminal glimpse of a scene from an old Western movie—a woman bouncing around on a buckboard, trying to hang on to a runaway team of horses.

Moments later, wrung out, boneless, all but brainless, he'd grinned like a damned fool while she slept on top of him. He'd thought about the sex. He'd thought about buckboards and runaway horses, about lessons he should have learned but obviously hadn't. Things he couldn't afford to think about now, if ever. And then he'd slept.

But not even the soothing sound of sleet on the windows and terrific sex could hold back reality forever. The best he could hope for was good news from Lyon. The next best was that, drained of excess tension, he might be able to think clearly and come up with some clue that had so far eluded him.

Ru stirred in her sleep, mumbling something. His arm was numb from the weight of her head, but he wasn't quite ready to let go. So he held her while he went over in his mind all the things he knew so far, all the things he didn't know, the few things they'd been able to rule out. He did his best to ignore the no-man's-land in between, but it was no use. Once his brain was engaged, the tension began gathering again at the base of his skull.

Quietly, with one lingering look at the woman sleeping beside him, he eased out of bed, flexed his shoulders and headed for the shower.

* * *

The news was no news. No new developments on the California end. Trav checked in with every contact on his list while Ru showered, dressed and cooked breakfast.

No deal. Nothing on the net, not that he'd expected anything.

He thought about all the kids' pictures he'd seen on milk cartons a few years back. Had that campaign worked? Did anything work when a kid decided to disappear?

Sharon insisted Matt had taken off on his own, but no one really knew for sure. So far there was no reason to believe he'd been kidnapped, but anything could have happened once he boarded that bus.

Swearing helplessly, Trav punched in his ex-wife's number again, and then had to wait for her to come fully awake. "Dammit, Sharon, I need a better picture to work with! That lousy snapshot you gave the cops—the way the sun hits his face, it looks like he's got a mustache!"

"Can I help it if he doesn't take good pictures? And stop yelling at me, I'm not your wife any longer, thank God, and besides, it's not my fault!"

Nothing was ever Sharon's fault. It wasn't her fault she'd gotten pregnant. It wasn't her fault she wanted more than he could provide. But it was her fault she was no longer his wife, and it was sure as hell her fault she'd forgotten to mention the small fact that he had a son. Forgotten, that is, until the kid started exhibiting a few behavioral problems at school.

At eight-ten he called Lyon's office, figuring he'd be there by now, and was eventually shuttled through to his private secretary, where he learned that Mr. Lawless was unavailable at the moment. After identifying himself as family, he was told that Mrs. Lawless had gone into labor, and Mr. Lawless was with her.

Evidently, something of his frustration and concern got through.

"You're his cousin, aren't you? Commander Holiday? Then you know she's three weeks early," the secretary confided. "The doctor doesn't think there's a real big problem, but all the same, you never know."

"No, you never do," Trav said, feeling as if the ground had just tilted under his feet.

"Mr. Lawless said he'd check in regularly, Commander. He said I should tell you that if there was anything new, he'd let you know. He'll probably call from the hospital as soon as he gets a chance. Oh, and he said to hang in there, that the waiting's the worst."

Trav hung up the phone, leaned back and flexed his shoulders. The waiting was the worst? God, he needed to believe that. Unfortunately he knew better. If there'd ever been a time in his life when he'd believed in happy endings, it was shoved so far back in his memory, buried under so much crap, there was no chance of ever retrieving it.

Ru came into the room. She neither tiptoed nor did she demand attention, simply placed a cup of coffee, well laced with milk, on the desk beside him.

"The trees are starting to ice up," she said.

He hadn't even glanced out the window yet. "Oh, hell," he said, thinking that if the power went off, there went his main link to the outside world. Chances were he'd still have a land line, but at a time like this, he needed all his resources.

"I don't take milk."

"I know. Drink it anyway, your stomach's probably pumping acid, you need the buffer."

He shot her a sour look, but took a sip, anyway. "I'd better go check on Miss Cal, see if there's anything she needs in case the road gets slick."

"Stay here, I'll go. I feel like getting out for a few minutes, anyway. If she needs something, I can stay here and man the phone while you drive to the store. I'm no good on icy streets with a stick shift."

Feeling a powerful need to do something—anything—he almost insisted on going himself, but reason won out. Just barely. Tipping the scales was the fact that he needed to be ready in case of power brownouts, a real possibility under the circumstances. His backup power would buy only enough time to close down his computer. If he lost his hard drive at a time like this, he'd really be up a creek.

"Wear something waterproof. I've got a slicker in the utility room. Tell her I'll be over sometime today to run the dog, and see if she needs any lamp oil, in case the lines go down. Oh, and Ru? Wear shoes that have some tread on the soles, will you? Chances are the ground'll be okay, but if you slip and break a leg, I don't have time to go find you."

It was as if the night had never happened. But they both knew it had. Sooner or later it would have to be dealt with, but right now he had other priorities.

"Hey," he said to her stiffly retreating back. "Watch your step, will you? I mean it."

As an apology, it was barely adequate. It fell woefully short of what he was feeling, but it would have to do for now.

Ru lifted her head, closed her eyes and inhaled deeply, savoring hints of salt, mud, winter-dried weeds and the resinous scent of freshly broken pine branches.

She liked the way things smelled here on the Outer Banks, so different from Atlanta, or even Lawrenceville.

She took another deep breath, warning herself not to hyperventilate, but needing to clear her head in order to think about what was happening to her.

It was the last thing she'd expected, or else she might have taken precautions. It had simply never occurred to her that she would fall in love. Certainly not in a place like this, with a man like Travis Holiday.

He was totally outside her experience. He might be an officer and a gentleman, but her mama would have been quick to point out that he wasn't "our kind of people." Verlie Roberts had always been something of a snob, in the nicest possible way, of course. Family meant everything, more than money. Even more than ethics.

She'd been nearly destroyed by the scandal, the loss of all she'd been brought up to believe in and hold dear. Whenever Ru was inclined to feel sorry for herself, she had only to think about her mother.

Hunching her shoulders under the weight of Trav's oversize foul-weather gear, she made her way carefully along the narrow path that twisted through gnarled live oaks, patches of bracken, catclaw briars and dead, broken pines, victims of wind and tide. Near the creek where the ground was inclined to be boggy, someone—probably Trav—had placed three planks. They were wet, but not frozen. Picking her way cautiously, she trudged up the ridge to the small frame house with the sagging front porch and the motley collection of fencing, still thinking about family. Hers and his.

She didn't know much about Trav's family, but she seriously doubted if any of his ancestors had belonged to the United Daughters of the Confederacy, or Sons of

Confederate Veterans, or even the League of the South. She'd been drilled from childhood in the importance of tradition, of upholding certain standards.

She had standards. She even believed in tradition, the South and the sanctity of marriage, but her beliefs had been sorely tested. In a scary, rapidly changing world, she wasn't certain they would ever fully recover, or if they even applied any longer.

What kind of tradition did Trav believe in? She had a feeling that, bone deep, he was every bit as steeped in tradition and duty as she was. She'd seen him at his worst—sick, unshaven, scared, miserable—ready to bite off her head at the least offense, or no offense at all other than being where she wasn't wanted.

Yet, even at his worst, she had sensed in him a strength she had never found in any other man. Maybe it was that elusive thing called character. Maybe it was the fact that before he'd ever touched her, she had wanted him to. Wondered what it would be like to make love to him. Wondered what he thought of her, knowing it couldn't be very flattering.

She was thirty-four years old, well acquainted with her few strengths and her many weaknesses. At her age, with her experience, one would think she'd have brains enough to stay out of trouble.

Sighing, she stomped the wet sand off her shoes and rapped on the door. "Miss Cal? It's Ruanna."

They visited for perhaps half an hour before Ru left with a grocery list and a promise that one of them would walk the dog before it got dark. Skye was evidently holed up in his snug house that consisted of a half-buried barrel under the southeast corner of the kitchen, surrounded by a fence constructed of slats, hogwire and weathered sheets of plywood. On a day like this, even a dog had sense enough to stay in out of the weather.

She called out to him on her way outside, forgetting that he couldn't hear her. ''See you later, boy. Trav'll be by to take you out for a run, okay?''

She was halfway up the ridge, marveling at the sheer beauty of the silent, ice-coated forest, when something caught her eye. A movement. In the premature gloom, with a curtain of freezing rain blocking out all but the immediate surroundings, any sort of movement would have caught her attention.

It was probably nothing, but she paused, waited a few seconds and then called out. ''Hello. Is anyone there?''

Silence.

Anxiety hovered just out of reach. It was nothing, she told herself again. Who in his right mind would be out on a day like this? All the same, she'd seen something—some movement—even if it was only a shadow.

''Whoever you are, if you go near the creek, watch out for the planks, they're starting to get slick.''

No reply, not that she'd expected one. It was probably a deer, maybe even a crow or some other big bird. Nobody with a grain of sense would be out walking in the woods on a day like this.

What about wild dogs?

''Don't even think such a thing,'' she muttered into her collar. Even a wild dog knew enough not to be out in this mess.

Clutching her coat tightly around her throat, she headed back up the ridge, looking forward to a mug of steaming Earl Gray.

Behind her someone sneezed. She froze.

Did animals sneeze? ''Look, if you're in trouble, you'd better speak up because I'm not hanging around outside a minute longer than I have to. This is getting really bad.'' Her voice was about as firm as a damp Kleenex. She blamed it on the cold, wet drizzle making its way down the back of her neck. ''I mean it. If you need help, say so. If not, I'm leaving.''

This time it was a whimper instead of a sneeze. And there was something awfully familiar about that particular low-voiced whimper.

''Skye? Is that you?'' Then she remembered that he couldn't hear her. She flexed her half-frozen fingers and tried to remember the hand signal for ''Get your mangy butt here this very instant!''

''Oh...my...God,'' she whispered as dog and boy crept out from under the sweeping branches of a giant cedar tree.

Ten

Ru's first impulse was to take them back to Miss Cal's house. They were roughly halfway between the two houses.

"Are you lost? What happened?" Skye was barking and prancing around her feet. The boy hung back, his look wary, frightened.

"Do you live around here?" He couldn't have come far. He wasn't dressed for the weather. No one in his right mind would be out in this mess wearing only a light windbreaker and threadbare jeans. And a backpack? Probably schoolbooks.

Did kids even carry books anymore, or had computers replaced them? "Look, if you missed the school bus, why not come home with me, and we'll call your folks to come pick you up."

He continued to stare at her. All she could see of his face between the turned-up collar and his rolled-down stocking cap was a pair of enormous dark eyes and a small, red-tipped nose.

Poor baby, he looked so cold and lost, she wanted to take him in her arms and give him a big hug, but a ride to his home would be a lot more welcome. Trav would know what to do.

She gave an exaggerated shiver. "Look, I don't know about you, but I'm freezing. I've got some hot chocolate mix. As for Skye..." She shook her head. "Been in the creek again, haven't you, stinky? I'll bet you dug out from under your fence."

"What did you call him?"

"Who, Skye, or stinky? He's called Skye on account of his blue eyes. Not that the sky's blue today. Where'd you find him? He's supposed to be penned up, but he's obviously been in that smelly old creek again."

Ru had begun to walk, hoping the pair would follow, not knowing what she would do if they didn't. Skye could probably take care of himself as long as there wasn't much traffic, but the child...

"He's deaf, by the way," she remarked, glancing back over her shoulder. "He knows hand signals, but first you have to get his attention. If he happens to be running away from you—well, you can see there might be a problem."

If she'd hoped to lure the child into talking—and she had—it wasn't working. He'd picked a lovely day to miss the bus. "Do you have a dog?"

He shook his head, the wary look never leaving his eyes.

"Well, this one's something of an escape artist. We think he knows how to pick locks, but we've never caught him at it. At any rate, his owner's going to want to thank you for catching him. Do you know Miss Cal? Oops—watch your shoestrings.''

He was wearing those hideous shoes all kids seemed to prefer these days, thick, clumsy, with the strings untied. Probably some sort of social comment. Each generation seemed to have its own means of rebelling against the previous one.

Silently he trudged along behind her, both hands crammed in his pockets. If he tripped on a shoestring, he'd land flat on his pretty face before he could catch himself, but she didn't think he'd appreciate being told how to walk in the woods safely.

Skye gave a sharp yip, darted around in front of Ru and then back to the boy, nudging each of them with a cold, wet nose.

''He's a herd dog. We're his herd. I think he's trying to tell us to stick closer together, stop dawdling and get in out of this messy weather. I can't much blame him, can you?''

For a boy who looked cold, scared and possibly lost, he tried hard not to show it. Probably bracing himself for what his parents were going to say when he was late getting home. ''Did you stay after school for a game or something?''

He shook his head. Or maybe he just shivered. She wanted to sweep him up in her arms and get him somewhere warm, but he wouldn't appreciate it, and she'd probably stagger into a tree and drop him. Lord knows what Skye would do. Tackle her, more than likely. The crazy mutt was inclined to be territorial.

''It's not far now. And look, if you're worried about Skye, then don't be. I'll call his owner and tell her where he is, and Trav—Commander Holiday, that is—he can call your folks and tell them where you are, and by the time they come to collect you, you'll be warm and dry and full of hot chocolate. Do we have a deal?"

"D-d-do you know my dad?"

Bingo. The kid had a tongue. "I'm afraid I don't know many people down here yet, honey, but my friend knows everyone on the island. Do you live in Buxton or one of the other villages?"

That solemn, brown-eyed stare again. "Never mind, let's get you warm and dry first, and then we can find out where you live." If there was one lesson she'd learned it was that, given the option, it was best to tackle one problem at a time.

"Here we are," she announced, sounding disgustingly chipper. For an unadorned shoebox, the house looked marvelously warm and welcoming, with lights glowing from every window. "Watch out for the steps. They weren't frozen when I came out, but the temperature's dropping pretty fast."

And then she was banging on the door, holding on to the lost child with one hand, in case he changed his mind about being rescued, and Skye's collar with the other—for more or less the same reason. She wasn't up to chasing either one of them if they decided to run. She needed a hand here.

"Travis? I've brought home company. You'd better get your rope." To the boy she said, "You might want to take your shoes off out here. I bet your socks are soaked, too, aren't they?"

She opened the door a crack and was stomping the sand off her own shoes when Skye gave a loud yap and shoved past her, nearly knocking her off her feet. "Come back here, you stinking animal," she yelled. "Grab him, will you, honey?" she said to the boy.

The boy lunged after the dog, leaving Ru gazing

helplessly at the trail of sand, mud and wet leaves across the once-gleaming floor. She shut the front door just as Trav emerged from the room she'd privately nicknamed the control tower.

From there, things went downhill. A tangled mixture of dog and boy crashed into a pair of long, jeans-clad legs. The boy landed on his butt and one elbow. Grinning from ear to shaggy ear, Skye planted his muddy front paws on Trav's clean shirt.

Trav stood his ground—just barely. The look on his face defied description. Slowly lifting his gaze to where Ru stood in the middle of the room, trying her best not to laugh, he said, "You want to give me a hint?"

"Look what I found. Or maybe they found me, I'm not sure. If you don't want Skye inside, and believe me," she added, wrinkling her nose as the smell of muddy, wet canine began to permeate the heated room, "I can understand if you don't, then I'll open him a can of ravioli and make him a bed on the back porch until you can take him home. I doubt if he'll stray far in this weather."

Trav felt a pulse begin to throb at his temple. The muscles at the back of his neck were already knotted. As the mixture of sleet and frozen rain beat fiercely against the outside of the house, emphasizing the warmth and silence within, he stared down at the kneeling boy, who was staring back up at him. In the melee, the stocking cap had come off to reveal a crop of dark, matted curls, a pair of enormous brown eyes and an olive-skinned face that was delicate to the point of being almost pretty.

A chilly feeling began to creep over him, much like a cold, rising tide.

"I guess I'm in pretty big trouble, huh?" the boy whispered.

"That depends," Trav said quietly, hoping he was wrong, knowing in his bones that he wasn't. "Just for the record, you want to tell me who you are and what you're doing here?"

The dog was everywhere, exploring everyone and everything in the room.

"Travis Holiday, where are your manners?" Ru's cheeks blazed with color. Her moss gray eyes blazed with anger. "This child is cold and wet, and you're acting like a truant officer! Do you think you might at least offer him something hot to drink and a dry shirt to wear until his folks can come for him? What's your name, honey? What's your phone number?"

One small arm crept around the dog, who paused to lap his face with a long, wet tongue. The boy lowered his gaze, and Travis turned to glare at Ru. "You don't get it, do you? Dammit, woman, where have you been these past two days?"

"Get what?" she wailed. "Travis, for heaven's sake, what's come over you? I know you're worried out of your mind, but that's no reason to—" Without finishing, she lunged for the dog. "Get off that sofa, you filthy mutt!"

Trav stomped on the floor. When the dog turned with a guilty look, he flicked a quick hand signal. Skye immediately slunk down off the rumpled denim cushions and flopped on the bare floor.

"Now then, Matthew," he said grimly, turning his attention back to the boy, "would you like to call your mother and tell her you arrived in one piece? She's pretty worried about you."

It took every shred of control at his command to keep

his voice even, his face expressionless, as, one by one, every hope and dream he'd built up since learning that he was a father collapsed around him. "There's the phone." He nodded to the portable. "You know the number. Tell her I'll put you on a plane as soon as the weather clears up. I'll let her know all pertinent data as soon as—"

"Travis Holiday! Stop it this minute, have you lost your mind?" Ru grabbed his arm and shook it. From his place on the floor between sofa and coffee table, Skye growled, but didn't budge. "Are you trying to tell me this is *Matt?* Your *son?* And this is the way you greet him? God, no wonder Sharon left you."

It took a lifetime of discipline acquired the hard way, but he only nodded. "Call your mother, Matthew. Then we'll see about getting you some dry clothes to put on."

"Don't you dare ignore me," Ru cried. "And you—Matthew—you stay right where you are. I don't know what's going on around here, but I darned well intend to find out."

Taking advantage of the distraction, Skye eased his considerable bulk up onto the coffee table, where he could be closer to the action. Ru continued to glare at Trav, who continued to glare back. He felt as if he'd aged a lifetime, but nothing of his feelings broke through the stern mask.

The boy mopped overbright eyes with a pair of grimy fists, leaving streaks across both cheeks. Trav had long since learned to ignore a woman's easy tears, but a child's tears—a boy's—he remembered too well how bitter those could be.

It was the noise of a growling stomach, loud in the unnatural silence, that broke the tension a moment later.

Trav snapped, "Go wash up, you might as well eat as long as you're here."

Ru pointed and said, "That way, honey. You'll find everything you need." Her tone of voice left no doubt as to whose side she was on.

Trav felt like bawling. It didn't help to remind himself that none of it was Matthew's fault. The kid couldn't help who his parents were—or who they weren't.

Sharon could wait, he told himself, stalking off to the bedroom to find something the kid could wear until his own clothes dried out. A few more hours of anxiety might do her good, give her a chance to sweat a little over all the lies she'd told.

It had all fallen into place the minute he'd stared down at those melted chocolate eyes, that crop of dark curls. He'd been stationed at Wildwood, New Jersey, at the time. Luis Galanos, half Latino, half Greek, had been the number-one heartthrob of every single woman on the base, and more than a few of the married ones. His own wife, included, Trav thought bitterly.

In a child those same flawless features were delicate, almost feminine. In a man they were lethal.

He'd heard rumors back then, but he'd chosen to ignore them. A military base, even when most of the personnel lived off base, was a closed community. Talk was cheap and plentiful. Most rumors were born of boredom, and the one thing he'd never been was bored.

But some of the wives had been bored, Sharon among them. He'd had no real objection when a few of the women loaded up a station wagon and headed to Atlantic City for a weekend of gambling. Beyond the occasional poker game, he'd never been interested in gambling. But then, neither did he consider it a cardinal sin.

Sharon had gone often. When he'd learned she was going alone, he'd suggested she might want to take up another hobby, one closer to home, but he hadn't pushed it. By then they'd been pretty much living as strangers. Polite, convenient housemates.

Sure, he'd heard the rumors. A friend of his reported seeing her in Atlantic City with Galanos, but when he'd confronted her with it, she'd claimed it was purely coincidental. They'd met by accident, and Luis had offered to show her how to play roulette.

Trav had actually gone with her one weekend, hoping to mend a few fences. To prove that he wasn't as dull as she accused him of being. It hadn't helped. Not the champagne, not the Jacuzzi, not the fancy king-size bed. Not even the sex.

He'd given it his best shot, but it hadn't been enough. Too late, too little. Three weeks later she'd walked out, and the next thing he'd heard, she'd moved to Nevada and filed for divorce.

Years later, when he'd all but forgotten he'd ever been married, she had tracked him down to tell him he was a father. That she'd been pregnant when she'd left him, thanks to that marathon weekend in Atlantic City.

It had taken him a while to get used to the idea. His first impulse had been to fly to California, where she was living with her second husband and their two daughters, and claim his son.

She'd nixed that idea out of hand. Give her a chance to break it to the boy, she'd said. After that it had been something else. They were getting ready to head out on vacation. The boy was having problems in school, and this wasn't the time to shake up his life. First one excuse, then another.

And he'd bought it. Oh, sure, he'd put through the

paperwork for an allotment so that at least he was supporting the kid. He'd started writing, sending pictures, making plans.

Building a house. That had taken a major chunk of his time and money over the past few months before he retired, but he'd wanted everything to be perfect when he brought his son home.

Fists crushing the black flannel shirt he held, Trav began to curse. The vein in his temple throbbed visibly.

Galanos. He'd been a civilian working at the Housing Office. Trav had known him only by sight and reputation. It hadn't occurred to him to blame the guy for the breakup of his marriage. That had been broken long before Galanos had come into the picture. But those were definitely Galanos's big, soulful eyes gazing up at him from Matthew's face, Galanos's dark, sloping brows.

Behind him the bedroom door slammed. Startled, he dropped the shirt. "Dammit, don't do that!"

"What in the world has got into you, Travis Holiday?"

"This doesn't concern you."

"It does so concern me! I brought that child here, and if you're going to treat him like a—a pariah—then I'll just take him somewhere else!"

"Fine. You do that. Maybe your friend Moselle's back in town."

Face drawn in anger, she crossed the floor and grabbed his arm in a punishing grip. "What's wrong with you? He's your son, the child you've been going out of your mind worrying over! Is that it? The strain was too much? Travis, how could you *possibly* treat any child, much less your own son, that way?"

Carefully he removed her hand from his arm. ''You don't know anything about it.''

''Then *tell* me! For God's sake, tell me what's going on!''

''Back off, Ruanna. This doesn't concern you.''

He might as well have struck her in the face. Steeling himself against feeling anything at all, Trav did what he had to do. ''See that he has a hot shower and something to eat. I don't want him getting sick and being stuck here.''

She looked mortally wounded. It didn't take long to figure it out, but by then it was too late. ''I didn't mean that the way it sounded, Ru, it's just that there are things you don't understand.''

''You're right. But I understand this much. You're so terrified of getting involved that you can't even risk it with your own child. There was never any risk where I was concerned, was there? When it comes to women, you're in no danger of weakening, but a son is different. Well, let me break the news to you—you can send him away now, but wherever he goes, he'll still be your son, and you'll never be able to forget that. I feel sorry for you, Travis, I really do.''

She left, closing the door quietly behind her. He wished she'd slammed it. Wished she'd punched him out, kicked him, screamed at him. Anything to crack though this cold, empty shell he'd spent so many years carefully erecting around his feelings.

Minutes after she left he still stood there, trying to deal with the pain by telling himself it didn't matter. God knew, it wasn't the first time he'd ever watched his expectations crash and burn. The trick was not to expect anything in the first place. Even an oyster knew better than to open himself up to risk. Touch any shellfish, and it snapped shut. At the first sign of trouble, a turtle knew enough to pull into its shell.

The danger was when you didn't retreat fast enough. When your reflexes were conned into relaxing, and you opened your shell and allowed someone else inside.

Kids' shells were thin. Some, the unlucky ones, never learned how to wall themself off securely.

Or maybe they were the lucky ones, the ones who had family to stand between them and trouble until they grew strong enough to survive alone. Kids like Matthew. Was he one of the lucky ones or one of the unlucky ones?

The shower was still running. He could hear Ru in the kitchen, slamming pots and pans, making the kind of noises a woman made when she was mad as hell and wanted the world to know it.

The shirt he'd been holding was far too big. Sized to accommodate his shoulders, with long tails meant to be tucked neatly inside his pants. Maybe a sweatshirt would be better. He found one rolled up in his bottom drawer. He was a roller, not a folder. Rolling was easier and took up less space. Maybe he'd tell the kid that, if he intended to do much more traveling with only a backpack.

Slinging the shirt over his shoulder, he ventured into the kitchen, half expecting to be bombarded with pots and pans. "What about this? Think it'll do?" He held up a gray sweatshirt.

"He might not need your charity. I doubt if he came three thousand miles without a change of clothes."

"It's not charity, dammit. And if he's got a change, it's probably dirty. He doesn't strike me as the kind of kid to spend much time in laundries."

"No?" She had silky, arched brows and knew how

to use them to best advantage. ''How does he strike you? A little too stupid to be an officer's son? Not quite up to standard? I believe you said Holidays ran to height, so you're right, he'll probably never make a great basketball player. But there are other sports. How about tennis? Or maybe even golf? You don't have to be tall to knock a tiny little ball into a hole in the ground. You don't even have to be all that brainy.''

She was obviously not ready to forgive him. He couldn't much blame her. ''Ru, don't be so quick to judge something you don't understand.'' No way was he going to explain. He still hadn't figured out how to tell the boy that not only had his mother been unfaithful, she had lied about it.

Oh, hell, he couldn't tell the kid that. Matt didn't deserve it. None of this mess was his fault.

Rubbing the back of his neck, he said tiredly, ''I'd better check in with Lyon and call off the chase.''

''What about letting his mother know he's safe? Matt never called her, you know.''

''Yeah, I'll do that, too, while I'm at it. If you think this shirt's all right, I'll reach in and hang it on the bathroom doorknob.''

Skye was back on the sofa. Trav didn't even bother to signal him onto the floor. What the hell difference did it make, it was only furniture.

He dialed Sharon's number and waited until the machine picked up. ''Sharon? Travis. I've got him. He's okay. I'll put him on a plane—direct flight if I can get one, but it might take a couple of days. The weather's lousy down here, and I'll have to drive him to Norfolk. He could probably do with a few days rest, anyway.''

Next he called Lyon's office and learned that the

Lawlesses had a little girl, seven pounds, two ounces, mother and child doing fine, father still in shock.

That, at least, elicited a smile. So much for the tough, hotshot federal agent. He left a brief, carefully worded message and remembered at the last moment to add his congratulations.

That done, he stood, stretched and said, ''Come on, you stinking hound, I'd better get you home before Miss Cal finds out you've run off. Take it from me, running away never solves anything. I guess I'm just going to have to build you a bigger pen.''

He poked his head into the kitchen. ''I'm going to take the dog back. Feed the kid, will you? I have a feeling he's running on empty.''

''How about looking in his bag before you go. As long as I'm washing what he was wearing, I might as well make a clean sweep.'' She was in flour up to her elbows. He didn't see why women had to make such a big deal about cooking. He'd been getting by for years with cans and Little Debbie's desserts.

''Yeah, I'll do that.'' Evidently, a truce was in effect. He only hoped it would hold until he could figure out what to do and how to accomplish it with the least damage all around.

The backpack had obviously been a good one, but it was long past its prime. Muddy, not to mention wet. Gingerly he unsnapped a flap and peered inside at a jumble of paper and underwear.

Ten minutes later he was still sitting on the sofa, the dog's muzzle on one knee, a stack of creased letters and photographs on the other. The dog whined. Absently Trav tugged on his ear.

As far as he could tell, the kid had brought along

every letter Trav had written him, from the one about rodeos in Oklahoma, to volcano-watching in Hawaii and red drum fishing off the point here on the island. Anything he thought might entice a boy into giving up the only home he'd ever known and throwing in with an unknown father.

He'd even written a few paragraphs about his mother's great-great-grandfather, old Squire Lawless, who'd built an empire on illicit whisky. Evidently the old guy had been a well-respected businessman in Tyrrell County. Colorful, at the very least. Trav had planned to take Matt to meet Lyon and Harrison, and any other Lawless cousins who happened to turn up. The lawyers had dug up a bunch of heirs and assigns.

Trav didn't know much about his father's side of the family, but on his mother's side there was more than enough to arouse a kid's curiosity. Moonshiners, bootleggers, tycoons, famous hunting guides, jailbirds, politicians. A legacy that covered so many generations could lead to a lot of interesting discussions, not to mention a few lessons in history and geography.

Education was important. With good grades and the proper recommendation, Matt wouldn't have had to fight his way up through the ranks. He'd have been a natural for the academy. Three generations of Coast Guardsmen would have been a pretty decent heritage for any kid.

His original mission forgotten, Trav rested his head on the back of the sofa, closed his eyes and sighed. Skye groaned and shifted to a more comfortable position, resting his muzzle on Trav's thigh.

"Dad?"

Dad. "Yeah, what is it, Matthew?" Feeling a hundred years old, Trav opened his eyes.

"Could I ask you something?"

"Sure, fire away."

Under the weight of a size forty-two sweatshirt, Matt squared his slight shoulders. "Does shaving with an electric razor hurt? The reason I asked, is Mom shaves her legs with one, but she says it pulls. My other dad has a beard. He gets a barber to trim it for him once a week."

"Is this something you need to know right away?" Trav played for time. The kid obviously knew there was something wrong, but if this was the way he wanted to handle it, Trav figured he might as well go along.

"I'm starting to get a mustache. If you look real close in a good light, you can see it." He edged closer to the lamp, tilting his face to reveal a fine dusting of peach fuzz on a smooth, olive complexion.

He hadn't got the soap out of his ears; his hair needed trimming, but as they were both feeling their way, Trav chose not to mention either thing. "Yeah, I see what you mean. Well, if you want to shave before you head back home, I can give you one of my razors and some shaving cream."

"I forgot my toothbrush, too. I chewed a lot of gum. Some lady told me on the bus that apples were good for cleaning teeth, so I ate a couple of those."

"Spare toothbrushes and disposable razors, second drawer, left-hand side."

The smile was cautious, testing the waters. "Thanks, I'll brush after I eat, then one brushing will last me for a while. But maybe I'll take a razor with me when I head back. Just in case I need it."

"Yeah, you do that," Trav said gruffly. He wanted to tell the kid not to be in such a hurry to grow up. And of all crazy things, he wanted to tell him not to be in such a big hurry to leave. ''As long as you came all this way, you might as well stick around a few days and do some sight-seeing.''

Matt glanced uncertainly out the window at the icy trees, the blowing branches, and Trav shrugged and said, ''Yeah, well...you picked a pretty rough time to show up. We don't usually get this kind of weather here.''

''Oh, no? Get him to tell you about the day I arrived, Matthew.'' Ru had dusted off the flour, but there was still a streak of something on the tip of her nose.

''Been snorting the cinnamon again?'' Trav challenged.

She took a swipe at her face, her eyes still guarded. ''If you two are ready to eat, I guess I'd better call Miss Cal and tell her I'll be over after supper with Skye.''

''I'll take him home,'' Trav said.

''Hey, can I go with you, Dad? He's a real neat dog, isn't he? Ru says he's deaf, but I think maybe he just hears what he wants to hear and tunes out the rest. Sometimes a guy has to do that, ya know?''

Trav nodded to the chair in the middle of the table and watched the boy slide into it, eagerly eyeing the platter of fried chicken Ru had rummaged from the freezer and microwaved. He looked as if he hadn't had a square meal in days. Ru had said he probably wouldn't be too critical.

Trav held her chair out, and when she slipped into it, his hands moved to her shoulders. Strong shoulders, for all they felt as frail as a bird's wing.

Were they strong enough for the road ahead?

Because he was going to need her. He still wasn't sure just how he was going to handle things, but one thing he knew was that he couldn't send the boy back to Sharon. He couldn't do that to any kid, and there was something about this one—

He remembered too well what it felt like to be that young, trying to shoulder burdens he didn't understand and shouldn't have had to carry.

Sooner or later he was going to have to tell him the truth, but not yet. First he'd give him time to adjust, to get his sea legs under him. Maybe when he was old enough to understand that the world wasn't black-and-white, that it was every color in the rainbow, plus a thousand shades of gray, he might try to explain.

Or maybe not. He was thirty-nine years old. There'd been more than a few times when he'd never expected to make it this far. Who knew how much farther he had to go? Who knew how far anyone had to go?

All he knew was that a steadying hand never hurt a boy, and the hand didn't necessarily have to belong to a father.

"Dad?"

He cleared his throat and took his place at the head of the table. "Yeah, Matthew."

"There's only two drumsticks. I guess you and Miss Ru want 'em, don't you?"

"Ru likes white meat. Me, I'm a wing man, myself." He avoided meeting Ru's gaze. His stomach growled. He said, "Why don't we split the take? A wing and a leg apiece, and Ru gets all the white meat?"

Matt's smile was still somewhat uncertain until Skye padded into the kitchen and plopped down beside his chair.

Ru wrinkled her nose and said, "Mercy."

"You asking or offering?" Trav retorted.

Their eyes met and held across the table. "Asking."

"Yeah, me, too." He was asking far more than he

knew how to put into words, but somehow she seemed to understand. Given time, maybe she could teach him to express himself better.

Given time—a lifetime—maybe they could make this thing work. Trav knew he'd never wanted anything so much in his life as he wanted these two people. Wanted them so much it scared him, made him want to laugh, to cry, to run like hell. He wanted to gather them up in his arms, dog and all, and hang on until his world settled down again.

But he didn't. Instead he said, ''Might as well set a few ground rules. We don't feed the dog at the table, else he'll be trying to eat from your plate.'' Matthew glanced quickly at Ru. She nodded. ''You can go with me to take him home while Ru makes up the cot in your room.''

Late that night, after the moon had broken through the clouds to cast lacework patterns on the bedroom wall, Trav tried to find the words to express what he was feeling.

''Ever wonder about the way things turn out? I mean, who'd have thought I'd fall for a woman who'd beat a helpless car to death with her shoulder bag?'' It didn't come close to expressing what he was feeling, but he was getting there.

Ru poked him in the ribs. ''You're never going to let me forget that, are you?''

''Nope. Any more than you're going to let me forget all the dumb things I said today.''

''Do you think he knows? About who his real father is, I mean.'' They'd talked about it. Trav had told her about Luis. She'd been furious, both on his behalf and Matt's.

"I doubt it. I can't see much point in trying to explain. It won't help him to know that his mother deliberately lied to him. That kind of thing gets a kid off to a bad start. He doesn't know who to trust, so after a while, he doesn't trust anyone."

"What about his stepfather?"

"It's hard to say. I get the feeling they're not too close, but he's probably a pretty decent sort. If two daddies, a mama and a stepmama—"

"A stepmama?"

A stricken look crossed his face. "You will, won't you? I mean, I just figured—"

"Of course I will. And by the way, in case you're interested, I do. Do you?"

Trav could feel the heat burning all the way up from the soles of his feet. "Yeah," he growled.

"Are you sure? Because I don't want to take any more chances."

Time to bite the bullet. "You're talking about love, I guess."

A strangled sound emerged from her throat, but he plowed ahead. "Okay, I love you. Anything that messes up my mind this bad has to be love. All I know is, I want you with me for the next fifty years. After that if you want to renegotiate, I'm game."

"And Matt?"

He thought about it, and then he said, "He's part of the bargain, Ru. I don't know if he's my son or not—biologically, that is. But I do know I can be a good father to him. I know all the wrong ways, and with you to help, I figure we can do things right and grow us a fine young man."

"Another mustang."

"Yeah, maybe."

"And maybe a daughter or two."

He laughed, but there was a choked sound to it, almost as if it hurt. "Definitely a daughter or two. Can't let Harrison and Lyon get ahead of us, not if we're going to establish a new dynasty."

The lighthouse swept over them, offering a silent blessing.

* * * * *

COMING NEXT MONTH

#1201 THE BEST HUSBAND IN TEXAS—Lass Small
Man of the Month
Austin Farrell was prime husband material—but he hadn't had a chance to prove that to Iris Smith. Now the widowed beauty was back in Texas and Austin was determined to lavish her with tender lovin' care. And prove that *this* cowboy was her destined husband-to-be!

#1202 JUST MY JOE—Joan Elliott Pickart
Gorgeous Joe Dillon was the stuff dreams were made of—especially Polly Chapman's dreams. But Polly knew that fantasies didn't always come true. Could Joe convince her that her dreams of marriage and family were possible—with him?

#1203 HIS SECRET CHILD—Beverly Barton
3 Babies for 3 Brothers
One sultry night, Sheila Vance lost herself in Caleb Bishop's arms. And unknown to him, Caleb became a father. Now the seductive bachelor was back and he had Sheila trembling—from passion and fear. Because Caleb was determined to find out what secret this mysterious beauty was hiding....

#1204 THE BRIDE MEANS BUSINESS—Anne Marie Winston
Butler County Brides
Jillian Kerr was never sure what to expect from Dax Piersall—hot, passionate embraces or cold accusations. Dax had left town years ago thinking Jillian had betrayed him. Now that he was back, could Jillian teach Dax to trust—and love—again?

#1205 EXPECTING...—Carol Grace
Pregnant Mallory Phillips had decided if she was going to live on Zach Calhoun's ranch, there were going to be some rules. No touching, no kissing, no passionate embraces! Of course, Zach set out to break every one of those rules....

#1206 THE BRIDAL PROMISE—Virginia Dove
Twelve years ago, Matt Ransom and Perri Stone had thought nothing would get in the way of their love. But family lies drove them apart. Now they are being forced to marry to save the land they both love. Can the truth of the past heal these two wounded hearts and make them one forever?